UNHOLY DYING

UNHOLY DYING

R.T. Campbell

Dover Publications, Inc., New York

This Dover edition, first published in 1985,
is an unabridged and slightly corrected republication of the work
originally published by John Westhouse (Publishers) Ltd, London,
November 1945, under the title *Unholy Dying: A Detective Story*.
R. T. Campbell is the pseudonym of Ruthven Todd.

Manufactured in the United States of America
Dover Publications, Inc.
31 East 2nd Street, Mineola, N.Y. 11501

Library of Congress Cataloging in Publication Data

Todd, Ruthven, 1914–
Unholy dying.

I. Title
PR6039.O26U49   1985   823′.912   85-10440
ISBN 0-486-24977-8

CONTENTS

PART ONE

PART TWO

PART THREE

APOLOGIA

An apology is due to all geneticists, none of whom, I am sure, would behave in the least like the characters in this book. It should not be necessary to state that all the characters are completely imaginary, and that any coincidence of name is pure coincidence.

PART ONE

CHAPTER 1

CONGRESS MEETS

THERE WAS SILENCE in the hall as the President rose to address the Congress. "Mr. Chairman, Ladies and Gentlemen," he said, speaking slowly and carefully, "I can hardly find words to express my feelings. I am overwhelmed when I think of the honour you have done me and how unworthy I am to occupy a position that has previously been occupied by so many much greater men. All that I can say is that it is my wish, and I will make every effort to turn that wish into an accomplished fact, to serve you, the Congress, in every way I can. Ladies and Gentlemen, I am your humble servant."

As he retired from the front of the stage and the clapping echoed round the vast dome, I looked around me, wondering how many different nationalities were gathered together to discuss their work, and I thought that, in addition to their many languages, they all were experts in one, that of science, of which I knew next to nothing. The things I knew about took place at least a hundred years before the study of genetics had become an organised science. The less reputable side of the late eighteenth century was my pigeon, the literary underworld of prophets who met the devil clad in a scarlet cloak strolling in the Tottenham Court Road and who claimed the Almighty as an uncle, of fantastic housemaids whose visions foretold the beginning of a new era of peace for mankind, and of mad artists who believed in the damnation of the body on earth.

My Uncle John was the reason why I was attending the 18th Congress of Geneticists. He is a botanist, or at least that is what I would call him, though I believe the correct term is a plant-physiologist, and once, when broke, I had managed to write an article on some stuff called colchicine with his assistance. This stuff, it seems, the juice of the autumn crocus, has the effect of making other plants produce new varieties of themselves when it is applied to them. I had sold this article to the *Daily Courier* and they must have liked it, for they had offered me the job of reporting the Congress. I rang up my Uncle John when I got the letter and asked him if he minded if I made a nuisance of myself by asking him damfool questions. His answering bellow had nearly split my ears, "Not the least, my boy, not the least. I'm only too glad to hear you're taking an interest in things that matter." His hoot of laughter echoed round the room for a long time after I had rung off.

So here I was seated among the scientists with whom I had nothing in common but a very healthy curiosity about everything. Owing to the fact that my Uncle John had paid out two guineas in hard cash I was not a journalist but a full-blown member of the Congress, due, some day, to receive a heavy volume of the proceedings, and, so long as I was not spoken to, I could pass as a scientist.

The first Plenary Session was just on the point of breaking up and about six rows behind me I saw my Uncle John, looking rather like a short-sighted baby elephant, struggling up from his seat, which he must have found a pretty tight fit, waving a large bundle of manuscript to his acquaintances around him and absent-mindedly ignoring the protests of his neighbours who, in the execution of this friendly gesture, he had swiped on their heads, to the devastation of the flora and fauna upon several professors' wives' hats.

I let the crowd pass by me and scribbled a few perfunctory notes on the back of an envelope, remembering that I was being paid to write a report of everything that might be of interest to the great general public. When the hall was nearly empty I got up and shoved my pen into my pocket.

Outside, in the Square, the members of the Congress had gathered into groups. In one of them I saw the huge beam end of Uncle John with the unpressed grey tweed trousers wrinkled round his knees and hanging baggily behind, adding to his resemblance to a young elephant. He turned his steel-rimmed spectacles towards me and blew heavily through his frayed moustache, which was white by nature but yellow by the grace of nicotine. He smacked me, rather too heartily, with the bundle of manuscript and boomed, "There was nothing there you couldn't understand, was there? It was all pap for the unweaned whelps."

"No, thank you," I said, "by concentrating hard I managed to take it all in."

He turned to his companions, saying, "You know my nephew,

Andrew Blake? He thinks his last name gives him a licence to be crazy."

I looked at the others as my uncle introduced them. Professor Silver was a small eager man with a cockatoo lock of greying hair which gave him the appearance of a shrunken version of Arnold Bennett, his voice was surprisingly harsh and I could not place his affected accent. Then there was a younger man, in grey flannels and a green tweed jacket, bound at the cuffs and elbows with chamois leather; he was addressed as Dr. Peter Hatton and, so far as I could judge at first glance, I liked his looks. The third was a puffy man, whose fat looked flabby opposed to the honest bulk of Uncle John, his eyes were deeply pouched and his mouth petulant and pinched at the corners. He acknowledged my uncle's introduction of him as Dr. Ian Porter with a Canadian drawl, "Waal, I guess I'd better be moving. Coming, Silver?" As I took the damp hand he rather grudgingly offered me, I thought of the phrenologists and wondered how the brain found room for itself in Porter's head, which was shaped like an inverted sea-gull's egg with all the width about the jowls.

"Uncle John," I said sternly, "you have not forgotten that you invited me to have lunch with you, have you?" He took a very short black pipe out of his pocket and stuck it in his mouth. Lighting it, to the immense danger of his moustache, with one of those old-fashioned fusees which explode like a volcano in eruption, he looked at me over the top of his glasses which had slipped half-way down his blunt nose, and scowled in a friendly fashion. "Since when, Andrew," he enquired, "have I been in the habit of forgetting my appointments?" I was just going to remark that if he did not forget them, he at least had cultivated a convenient habit of ignoring them at will when he continued, "At any rate, my luncheon appointments? You don't mind, do you, if young Peter here eats with us? You'll find him useful for he's a proper geneticist, not a dabbler like myself."

He laughed gustily and so loud that the attention of the other groups was focused upon us for a moment. "That's very kind of you, Professor Stubbs," said Dr. Hatton, with the air of one who was hearing about the invitation for the first time. My uncle stumped across the square, brandishing his bundle of papers at such of his friends as he encountered. I fell into step with Hatton and explained that I was a journalist in scientist's clothing, a lamb who would only too easily be led astray, and that I hoped that he would not pull my leg too much if I asked questions that were so simple as to be beneath his notice. He said cheerfully that he would promise not to mislead me more than he felt right, if in return I would promise not to ask him whether he could foretell the sex of an unborn infant or whether he could produce human twins at will. These questions were apparently the favourites among journalists and I said that I would refrain from asking them unless I found that he had led me along the garden path to the maze.

Uncle John was approaching his car, a vehicle so remarkable that it deserves some special notice. It was an immense Bentley of extremely uncertain age, reminding the beholder of nothing so much as one of those vast old four-poster beds one finds in show palaces. I always expected to find an iron step of the sort used to help one mount into a dog-cart, but Uncle John, with a nimbleness surprising in a man of his bulk, swung the starting handle and scrambled on board before the car had time to run away. He told me once that he had learned to do the winding-up and jumping after the car had run away one day in Oxford and he had been forced to commandeer a bicycle and chase it down St. Giles, catching it only about ten feet from some pile of notable stone. He had had very little doubt that, if it had felt so inclined, his Bentley would have demolished Oxford as a kind of hors d'oeuvre and continued to do the same by Cambridge for an entrée.

Conversation in this car was an impossibility. All one could do was to hang on to the sides and hope for the best, thanking God that there was no boom to swing over suddenly and catch you a crack on the side of the head when Uncle John brought her to, rather too suddenly. Uncle John concentrated on his driving with the grim concentration of a chessplayer. I have an idea that he really is rather frightened of it, but is determined that he will show it who is the master. His idea of showing it consists of driving as fast as he can and braking just in time to avoid disaster.

Whenever it seemed that the Bentley had successfully jumped over a Baby Austin or had contracted to a width of eighteen inches to squeeze between a lorry and a bus, Uncle John glanced up to heaven as if to thank it and, releasing one clutching hand from the wheel, snatched a large red bandana handkerchief from his pocket and rubbed it across his glasses. I held my breath during his prayers and the intervals when his sight was obscured by the gaudy handkerchief, but it seemed that his prayers were always answered and that he must have had a private treaty with heaven, for nothing out of the way happened—a few skids on tram-lines and terrified cyclists could hardly count.

At last, after a drive that seemed to have lasted for ten years, we drew up outside the best hotel in Gowerburgh. Drew up is, perhaps, hardly the right phrase, for stopping with Uncle John implied a great deal more than that; the skilful use of a snaffle seemed to attend the ceremony in spirit. I could have imagined my uncle calling for an ostler to rub his steed down and give it a bran mash. As it was he beckoned to Hatton and me to dismount. We climbed out of the back where we had been perched on bundles of books, books of all sorts—from detective stories and biographies to scientific works and bound copies of periodicals. We drew a large tarpaulin over this cockpit in case it rained and followed Uncle John into the White Lion.

He was already seated at a table in the dining room, with three glasses of sherry in front of him, reading a detective story by John Dickson Carr. We sat down and he looked up. "I've ordered the food," he said, "boys of your age don't know what to eat in a place like this. In a pub like this you should never get anything with a French name, it only covers the fact that they are using up the things that were left over from yesterday." The waiter, who was standing by, smiled at this slanderous statement. "What would you like to drink, sir?" he asked, holding out the wine list.

Uncle John smiled villainously up at him as he pushed away the book. "Beer. You don't imagine I'm going to ruin my digestion drinking your vinegar disguised as Chateau this and Chateau that, do you? Three pints of bitter."

While we ate a mixed grill I asked my uncle about Professor Silver, trying to hide my faint distaste from him. It was no use. "Ah, ha," boomed Uncle John, "you don't like him, do you? Well, you're not the only one, but he's a clever man all the same. A walkin' inferiority complex, that's what he is. He's just finished writin' a vast book about everything and is determined that it'll out Hogben Hogben and leave Haldane and Huxley in the slim volume class. Don't tell him I said this or he'll never talk to me again," he grunted gustily and went on, "or at least until he wants something from me."

I glanced around and saw that the people at all the tables near were listening to my uncle; he saw me looking at them but continued as loudly as before. "Oh, I don't mind him. The poor devil doesn't know what he wants, except that he wishes to be famous and he hopes that the *Compendium of Knowledge* will establish him, and that it will be a tombstone over his forgotten bones. The person I can't stand is his familiar spirit, Porter. I'd rather have a glass of stout any day." He hooted at his pun and then caught my severe glance and looked down at his plate for a moment, as if slightly ashamed. It was half a minute before I realised that he was still laughing, either at his own joke or at me. He looked up again, his face normal. "Porter's a nasty devil if you want one. And there are a lot of people who would be glad to see him in his grave. I, for one, would be pleased to send a wreath, how about you, Peter, eh?"

Peter Hatton scowled and muttered "I'd like to kill the bastard, always shoving himself in where he's not wanted." This was above my head so I looked for an answer in the bottom of my tankard. When I came up for air my Uncle John looked at me and said, "Oh, there you are, Andrew? I thought we'd lost you. Don't you worry yourself about our likes and dislikes, they have nothing to do with your job and however much reason Peter has for dislikin' Porter I don't think you'll find him stickin' a lancet between his ribs."

For the rest of the lunch Uncle John and Peter tried to teach me something about heredity. I was not a very apt pupil, but I managed to get a rough idea of the Mendelian theory after they had illustrated it for me on the table with matches, some in their original purity and some dipped in the mustard. After they had finished with this I showed them how to make a tripod with three matches, strong enough to support a tankard of beer. Uncle John managed to do the trick at his first try and, just to prove how strong the tripod was, he had the tankards filled up again, explaining that the empty ones were not giving the trick a fair chance.

We had coffee and liqueurs and then Uncle John rubbed his hands together joyfully. "I'll drive you two boys up to the University," he announced with pleasure at the thought of showing off his charger once again, "and Peter will show you round, John, and then he'll tell you a bit about what he's doin'. I've got one or two people I must see."

Peter and I jammed ourselves in between the books and cowered down, feeling that it was perhaps safer to be inside the cockpit than sitting on its edge, for at any rate by doing this we avoided risk of being shaken off. I had my mouth open when the Bentley started and it was quite a time before I could manage to shut it, owing to the pressure of the wind.

The University of Gowerburgh had handed over the whole of several departments, Chemistry, Biology and Zoology, for the use of the Congress, and these in turn had been divided up into lecture rooms, demonstrations and exhibits. Peter, rightly judging that I would get the greatest amount of instruction out of the exhibits, took me round these. I looked into innumerable microscopes at strange brightly coloured landscapes with objects that looked like stuffed caterpillars. These were called chromosomes, Peter told me, and, so far as I could make out, they contained unknown objects called genes. Each characteristic I possessed was apparently due to the fact that I had a gene ordering me to possess it. I had blue eyes because I had the gene for it, my hair was dark because I had the gene for it, and it seemed that I had inherited these genes from my parents, who in turn had inherited them from their parents and so on right back to the beginning of history when my first ancestors were bits of jelly in a pond. I thought of the mediaeval idea of the homunculus and wondered whether it had not been nearer to the truth than the ages of enlightenment had allowed.

Peter got so carried away by the process of inheritance that I became quite depressed to think that I had nothing that was not present in my ancestors. There did not seem to be much point in being an individual. Peter noticed my depressed features and laughed. "What's the matter, Andrew?" he said, "finding all this above your head?" I shook my head and explained my thoughts. "Oh, that's all right," Peter said, "you are a biological necessity." He then proceeded to tell me about mutations in genes which apparently meant that sometimes breeding was not true but that for some unexplained reason a freak was born who had qualities that were not present in either parent. I did not like to think that if I had any individuality it was as the result of my being a freak and I told him so and he went on to wound my vanity even further by telling me that, after all, I was only something frothed up around an egg, by that egg in order to guarantee its continued existence. Having reduced me to the level of a milk-shake, Peter took pity on me and suggested that I might like a cup of tea. I wondered whether the hot tea would not melt the froth but decided I would risk it.

We walked across a lawn to the students' union which had in honour of the occasion been turned into a café for the use of the members of the Congress. We went into the tea-room and Peter looked around him anxiously. A girl in a white overall waved to him and we went towards her. I did not know whether I was included in her wave so I lagged behind and was going to sit down at an unoccupied table when Peter said, "Come on, froth, don't melt before you get your tea." He introduced the girl as Mary Lewis and me as a frothed-up egg who was feeling worried about it. I thought the joke was beginning to pall and was glad when he turned to his companion. "Well, Mary," he said, "how've things been this afternoon? Has that swine Porter been around?"

She hesitated for a moment and then said, "Yes, he's been fussing about all the time. Telling us all how to do things and explaining how he would run things if he was in charge. Thank God he's not in charge. Old Silver's bad enough, but Porter would be ten thousand times worse."

Peter looked at her and his lower lip tightened. "I can't stand the way he comes up to you, Mary," he said, "and puts his dirty arm round your shoulder while he looks to see what you're doing. One of these days I'll crack him one in the middle of his fat face." The thought seemed to please him and he smiled as he rubbed his knuckles.

"Now, Peter," Mary said, "he's not as bad as all that, you know. His manner's against him and he can't help it. I'm sure he doesn't realise that he's being unpleasant."

I cowered down out of the draught as Peter snorted, "Oh, no, he's not bad, is he? It's just his unfortunate manner, is it? I suppose he can't help stealing the credit for other people's ideas, can he? What about your pet *drosophila sub-obscura*? Who wrote the article about them in the *Journal of Genetics*? You know you did, but your name did not appear at all. It was all a contribution to science by that brilliant young geneticist—Doctor Ian Porter."

Mary smiled and said, "Well, I *was* working under him, wasn't I? Anyhow, Mr. Blake must be finding this discussion very dull." I changed this subject by asking them what *drosophila* was. "The vinegar-fly to you, old boy," replied Peter, appearing to forget his thoughts about the unpleasant Dr. Porter. "It has a new generation once a fortnight and so we can have in a year the same amount of development that would occur in a couple of centuries of the history of mankind. It's a nice thought, isn't it, that we know more about a little red-eyed fly, no bigger than a match head, than we know about any other creature on the face of the earth?" He paused and continued reflectively, "I wonder what kind of ancestry produced Porter." Mary looked at him warningly and said, "Now, Peter." He looked over his shoulder and, following his eyes, I saw Porter approaching, with Professor Silver behind him, like an adoring terrier.

Porter looked at us insolently and drawled, in his mock-Oxford Canadian accent, "Hullo, Hatton and Mr. Whatsyername." "Blake," I supplied obligingly, but he ignored me and went round the table to the place where Mary was sitting. She frowned at Peter who seemed to me slightly white around the temples and whose hands, beside me, were clenched so tightly that his knuckles were the yellow of old paper. Porter put his arm on Mary's left shoulder and then sat down in the chair at her right, so that his arm was across her shoulder. Professor Silver sat down quietly beside me and said something I did not hear as I was too occupied in the scene across the table.

Mary Lewis tried to disengage herself from the arm round her shoulders but Porter's fingers tightened on her overall. She turned her eyes on Peter as if commanding him to remain seated and then looked round. "Dr. Porter," she said coldly, "I would rather that you didn't put your arm round my shoulder."

I thought the whole affair was developing into a melodrama and, while I can stand my melodrama on the stage or in one of my favourite gothic novels, I do not feel comfortable when I am, however remotely, mixed up in it, so I dug in my pocket and found a packet of cigarettes. Putting on my best silly-ass, fools-walk-in expression I offered them to Mary. She looked surprised but took one. "Dr. Porter?" I asked, holding them so that he could not reach them with his free hand and was forced to take his arm off Mary's shoulder to pick one out of the packet. I thought for a moment that he was going to ignore the Player's I was holding out, then he relaxed and, removing his arm, took a cigarette. Mary moved round the table to light her cigarette from the match Peter offered her and, when it was going, she sat down in the vacant chair beside him.

Although the atmosphere felt a little less like that of a ruined monastery on a thundery night with the bats dipping around and the headless abbot on the prowl, there was still a good deal of tension about and I think I have rarely seen as much hate bottled in any glance as I saw in the one Peter threw at Porter. I know that if I had been Porter I would have felt that I would not, under any circumstances, meet Peter alone. The only person who seemed to be unaware of the thick atmosphere round our table was Professor Silver, who was grating away at my side about the unfamiliarity of my surroundings and who offered to help me if he could. He gave me the impression that despite his diffidence there was no one present at the congress who could help me like Professor Silver. I thanked him for his kind offer and he seemed genuinely pleased to think that I was not hostile towards him, and moved on to the subject of my uncle.

"I have known your uncle, Professor Stubbs," he said, "for a considerable number of years. He's a very brilliant man but lacks the concentrated drive and he is always running off after some wild idea or other. All the same, I must admit he has made some contributions, some excellent contributions. But it's a pity that he doesn't stick to the one thing. You know the old saying about a cobbler sticking to his last?"

By inclining my head towards him I indicated the fact that I did, indeed, know the old saying and I thought of my Uncle John and the pleased way he would have puffed out his moustache if he had been able to overhear Professor Silver trying to pinch him into a pigeon-hole. I determined that I would tell him all about it on the first possible occasion, and I would also suggest that he dropped Porter a word of warning about the fate of those who walked on gunpowder barrels with lighted matches in their hands. I did not think that I would like to see Peter up in court on a charge of assault.

Porter was pulling heavily on his cigarette and he leaned forward. "Mr. Whatsyername, you're a nephew of Professor Stubbs, eh?" he said. "Blake. Yes," I replied; I do not know why it was but the fact that he could not remember my name annoyed me so much that I felt that I would quite gladly join Peter in a party to beat him up. I think the reason that this trick irritated me was that I felt it was deliberate insolence, for on neither occasion had there been any real need for him to address me by name at all, a look in my direction would have been sufficient to draw my attention to the fact that he was speaking to me if he had really been quite unable to remember my name, which I doubted, as it did not seem to be a difficult one to recall, certainly no harder than Porter.

"Funny old boy, isn't he?" Porter continued. "I can never understand what he's doing playing at being a scientist. He's no more a scientist than I am a magpie." I heard a faint laugh from Peter at my side, but, fortunately, the sound did not reach across the table. He rolled on undisturbed, "He knows a little about everything but nothing much about anything." He seemed pleased with his remark and paused. The voice of Professor Silver scraped its way into my consciousness. "Now Ian," he was saying, in a tone of mild and affectionate rebuke, "that's hardly fair. I was just telling Mr. Blake that his uncle had made some very real contributions and that we scientists regretted his multitude of side lines. Don't you agree with me, Ian?" He seemed to be begging for agreement and smiled as if he had received a kindly pat on his head when Porter looked at him a little sourly and said, grudgingly, "Well, Silver, I suppose I will allow you that, but you can't deny that he's got a mind like a magpie and is a picker up of the unconsidered trifles left by other and better men. That he manages to make anything out of them is just his luck. Then he's not a serious scientist but an actor. Look at that car of his. He just has it for effect. Look at that pipe he smokes. Look at his clothes. Everything about him shows that he's just an actor and not a very good one at that."

Peter and Mary rose, and the former said, "Coming, Andrew?" I got up and nodded to Silver and then to Porter. "We'll continue the subject of your uncle another time," he said, "if you like, Mr. Whatsyername." "Blake," I muttered automatically and turned my back.

CHAPTER 2

CONGRESS DANCES

I HAD DINNER with Uncle John at the White Lion. I told him about the opinions I had collected concerning his character and abilities. He sucked at the large cigar he was smoking and, removing it, blew a series of smoke rings, the sight of which made him chuckle like a child that had just succeeded in blowing its first soap-bubble. "Of course they're right," he bellowed. "Other people are always right about one. I know I'm lazy and that I pick up the ideas that other men have long ago discarded. But they only give you one side of the picture. I want to see why the ideas were discarded, what went wrong with the works and whether I can't find a way round the difficulty."

He lay back in his chair and his snorts crashed like a thunder among the palm-trees and the alcoves of the lounge. Then he leaned forward and looked at me, grinning fiendishly, "I like the idea of Porter," he remarked, "saying I was a thief of other men's ideas. It's Caliban seeing his face in the mirror. The man himself lives by what he steals. Of course, he's never stolen anything from me, except my best remarks, and I can't really object to that, though I do get annoyed when he spoils them. But he steals from his assistants and from Silver, his assistants are under him and they will remain anonymous just as long as he can keep them anonymous. Of course, in his way he's a good teacher and he knows it and considers that any ideas that occur to those under him are his just reward for the things he is doing for them. Naturally, they can't be expected to see things in this light and sooner or later they object to it and then there's a hell of a row and out they go and they've no redress. But on the other hand there's old Silver. He doesn't mind what Porter steals and, in fact, I don't think he even notices that Porter is stealing from him."

For a few minutes he lay back and smoked in silence, his barrel chest, bound with a thick gold watch chain like a hoop, rising and falling rhythmically. His eyes were shut and I wondered vaguely how he enjoyed smoking when he could not watch the smoke curling up. I had noticed this habit of smoking with closed eyes previously and knew that it was not just a trick, but that, somehow or other, Uncle John found that his thoughts became clearer with something in his mouth and his eyes shut.

He opened one eye and looked at me and then he shut it again. For a full minute, by the clock behind him, he did not seem to breathe. Then he sat up and shook himself vigorously, knocking three-quarters of an inch of cigar-ash over his waistcoat and trousers. With a blunt hand he made a gesture of sweeping the ash off himself, a gesture that merely served to rub the ash down in a long dirty white smear.

"Humf," he grunted. "What you tell me about young Peter worries me. I've always said that Porter will get his head knocked in for him some day, but I wouldn't like one of my friends to be hanged for the deed. I'd rather do it myself than let that happen, for if I murdered him they wouldn't know it was a murder. The old man's got some tricks up his sleeve, but he hasn't applied his talents to murder—not yet. I'd rather it was one of the others, though, that did Porter in and I can't say that I'd blame anyone who did it. I've often felt I'd like to myself. But it's his damn superiority gets me, not his stealin' habits. However, he'd better watch out. It's one thing to pick a man's brain and another to try to steal his woman."

He heaved himself out of the easy chair and a small cascade of dead matches and cigar-ashes tumbled off him on to the floor of the lounge. He planted one of his wrinkled brown brogues firmly on the heap of debris and it crunched briskly. "If we're going to that reception," he remarked, "we'd better start." He pulled heavily on his rat's tail of a tie, making it look more like an unravelled bit of string than before, and ruffled his mop of grey hair into an untidy tangle. I sat beside him in the high front seats of the Bentley as we roared and rattled our way towards the University and the dance which was being given in the common-room.

I had hoped that Porter would not be at the dance but he was standing beside the bar with a glass of whisky in his hand, wearing a dinner-jacket. My uncle turned to the bar and ordered a couple of Johnny Walker's. Porter fixed his eyes on me. He was slightly drunk and his goldfish eyes were protuberant and looked as though they were made of misty glass or had developed some fungoid affliction. "Oh, hullo, Stubbs," he said thickly, "and you too Mr. Whatsyername." I looked at him as coldly as I could and barked at him. "The name's Blake. B-L-A-K-E. Could you try to remember it, *Mister* Porter."

He growled at me and lobbed his fat body nearer. "What y'say?" he demanded, "Say't again." "I said my name was Blake, *Mister* Porter!" "'Re you looking for a fight," he demanded again. "No," I replied, "were you?" He leaned over me and stuck his nose within an inch of mine. "Well, then you be careful what you say, Mr. Whatsyername." The smell of second-hand whisky was almost overpowering. "All right, *Mister* Porter," I answered, soothingly. He lifted his hand and flicked me on the ear, sharply.

I did not mean to hit him hard and merely tapped him on the solar-plexus. It must have been something to do with the amount he had drunk, for he just fell down and rolled over. I thought I had hurt him seriously and bent over him. My Uncle John pushed me aside and lifted Porter's eyelids. "Ha," he said, laughing softly, "he's fallen asleep. The best thing he could do."

In the background the voice of Silver was like the scraping of a double-bass, scratching away in the silence that had fallen upon the room. I looked round and got the impression that I had fallen into the middle of a Bateman drawing, the man who did something wrong; the eyes were like black paper discs and the open mouths seemed to have been frozen in the middle of an alleluiah, by a hard snap which had turned the sounds to icicles. My uncle did not seem to be aware that he was doing anything out of the ordinary as he removed Porter's black bow and unstudded the stiff front of his white shirt. He looked up at me over his shoulder and said, "Give me a hand with him, Andrew, and we'll put him over by the door. A couple of hours' sleep should make him all right, or as all right as he'll ever be."

I took hold of Porter's ankles and Uncle John gripped his shoulders. He was surprisingly light considering his flabby fatness, and we laid him in an armchair to the corncrake screeching of Silver. The band started and the open mouths clapped shut and the hanging arms were once more draped about their partners. We went back to the bar to get our drinks. My Uncle chuckled deeply and roared, in a voice that seemed to make the dance band, with all its hot drummers and swinging saxophones, sound like a radio with a run-down battery. "Ha, you've done what a lot of people would've liked to do and you didn't mean to do it."

One thing rather worried me and that was the behaviour of Professor Silver. He was running backwards and forwards between the comatose figure in the armchair and the bar, where he ordered double whiskies and drank them very fast. I felt rather sorry for him and moved towards him the next time he came to the bar, in order to tell him that I had not intended to knock Porter out and that I had no quarrel with him personally. However, when I opened my mouth he took his glass in his hand and zigzagged down the room, dodging between the dancers like a wounded woodcock.

I stood looking after him and did not see Peter and Mary approaching until he tapped me on the shoulder. "Hullo, Andrew," he said. "You're looking as if you'd just seen a ghost. What's the matter with you?" I tried to explain what had happened. My explanation was punctuated with grunts, chuckles and snorts from Uncle John, while Peter looked at me enviously. "My God," he said, addressing an invisible audience, "here's a chap whose just done what I've been restraining myself from doing all day and he has the nerve to suggest that he's sorry he did it. I'd be sorry I hadn't hit a lot harder and killed the swine."

In reply to this I pointed out that I personally had no quarrel with Porter except his inability or unwillingness to remember my name and that I had probably insulted him more than he had insulted me, by my insistence upon Mister rather than Doctor. I was willing to admit that Porter was an unpleasant specimen and that perhaps the world would be a better place for his absence than it was while honoured with his presence, but I deprecated the suggestion that I should be the instrument of his departure to tropical regions. I felt my neck and said that, so far as I could make out, it was already long enough and that, anyhow, it suited me without being stretched.

When I paused for breath my Uncle John, on whom the whisky was having a mellowing effect, started clapping loudly and shouting for an encore. The noise he made nearly deafened me and caused the band to stop abruptly in the middle of a waltz. He looked puzzled and in a whisper as loud as the growl of an enraged bear, "Why have they stopped? Is anythin' wrong?" The band apparently decided that there was nothing much the matter except that a member of their audience had gone mad, so, after the leader had turned a severe look in our direction, they started the waltz again.

Uncle John appeared to be suffering some remorse for his interruption of the dancers, for his voice was no louder than a normal man's shout as he turned to Mary. "Miss Lewis," he said, bowing towards her, "in my youth I used to be able to waltz a little. Are you willing to risk it with an old man whose feet are perhaps not as nimble as they used to be?"

Mary smiled at him and he took her hand and led her on to the floor. Peter and I watched them for a moment. The bulky figure of my uncle swung to the rhythm of the waltz with an ease that I would not have suspected him capable of. We turned towards the bar and I ordered beer, feeling that any further indulgence in Johnny Walker would have a definitely bad effect upon my sobriety and, as my Uncle's guest, I thought it was incumbent upon me to behave in a sober and proper manner. I smiled as I thought of the propriety of my evening's behaviour. I had first insulted and then knocked out a scientific member of the Congress. Peter looked at me and said, "Look here, I'd like to thank you for this afternoon. Your silly ass act prevented me making a fool of myself, for I was just on the point of getting up and taking a swing at the swine and it wouldn't have done any good." He paused and sighed, "I'm afraid though that I'll take a proper wallop at him one of these days and I won't know where to stop. I'll just go on banging at him till he falls apart or until they take me away and shut me up in a padded cell. I'd like to have been here when you hit him and to have seen him fall." He looked serious as he went on, "I'm rather ashamed to admit it, for I thought I had my feelings under better control, but when I think of Porter I go blood-crazy. You know these stories about native tribes and how the drumming sends them mad and they'll kill anything in their path? Well, that's how the repetition of Porter's name gets me. Just as the natives retain a verge of sanity which prevents them killing their own tribesmen, so I retain enough sanity to hate only Porter, but all my hate is focused upon him, my hate of other people seems to have been transferred to him. One of these days I'm afraid I'll kill him and that'll be the end of it."

I tried to look like an elder brother, one of those people who always understands, as I replied to him. "Peter, the trouble is Mary, isn't it? Well, then, if she can manage to stand him and I don't think you need be afraid of her having any deeper feeling than that of tolerance, why can't you ignore his behaviour. After all you don't need to see him very often. I know that you are working in Newcastle while she is one of his assistants in London, but even then you manage to get up to town fairly frequently, and she won't go on working with him for ever. If I were you I'd keep out of his way as much as possible."

This advice was, I knew, no more use than any friendly advice ever is, but I hoped that Peter would not cut loose at Porter, for the ensuing fracas would do neither of them any good professionally. The fact that I had knocked him out did not matter, for I was a crazy journalist, and as all journalists, on account of the films, have a reputation for perpetual drunkenness, it could be explained that I was roaring tight and had been looking for trouble. The waltz finished and Mary and Uncle John returned to the bar.

We talked trivialities for a few minutes and then my uncle boomed, "Well, Andrew, your neck won't be elongated this time. You haven't killed him." I turned round and saw Porter, his face the colour of the moon, weaving his way through the dancers and pushing aside the offers of assistance which he was receiving from Silver who was hopping along at his side like an excited parakeet. His tie was hanging loosely from the flapping wings of his collar and his blue silk underclothes were visible through the buckled starched front of his shirt. His eyes were fixed as though he had lost the power of moving them and his long white damp hands hung like rubber gloves filled with wet sand. His feet were splayed to take the swaying weight of his body.

I wondered whether he was returning to hit me. I hoped not, for he did not look as though he was in any condition to fight anyone, even his own shadow, let alone a sober man such as I was. Half turning to Uncle John, but keeping the uncertain figure still in view, I asked him some silly question about the evening primrose, the plant he was an authority upon, and, obviously seeing what I was doing, he gave me a long and involved reply which I did not hear. Mary was whispering to Peter, and I guessed she was telling him not to make a fool of himself.

Porter paid no attention to our group but laid himself limply against the bar and muttered, in a phlegm-clogged voice, "A large gin and tonic." The barmaid looked at him doubtfully, but, as she had obviously received no instructions about refusing drinks to drunken scientists, she served him with the drink, diluting it thoroughly with the quinine. He sipped it slowly and as if he was imbibing the elixir of life his dead eyes came slowly to life again and swivelled round the room until they came to rest on us.

I laid down my glass of beer as he moved along the bar, supporting himself on hands like dead starfish. He drew himself up as straight as he could and bowed slightly, but I could not tell if the bow was due to politeness or a sudden nausea. "Mr. Whats-er-Blake," he corrected himself, "my friend, Professor Silver informs me that I owe you an apology. If that is so I wish to tender it." I felt uncomfortable and mumbled, "Oh, that's all right, Doctor Porter." His body shook, like an immense jelly, under the impact of a hiccup as he turned away from me, apparently convinced that he had (in capitals) Done The Right Thing. His sway carried him over to Mary, who looked up as his shadow obscured the electric lights. "Mary," he drawled, looking aside at Peter as if at a bit of dust on his sleeve, "will you dance with me?"

Peter looked explosive and I saw my Uncle John's thick fingers tighten round his arm. I am not a very quick thinker but it occurred to me that Porter had received enough knocking around for one evening and I pushed myself forward. "Sorry, Doctor Porter," I said, "Miss Lewis has promised me this dance and I heard my uncle ask her for the one after."

He looked at me without expression and said with drunken preciseness, "All right, Mr. Blake. I think I understand you." He swung round so hard that I thought he was about to start revolving like a gyroscopic top and, collecting Silver like a burr, swayed once more towards the door.

My Uncle John's fingers were still fastened like claws on Peter's sleeve and he was rumbling away in an undertone, "It's not worth it, boy. You'll just cause yourself and Mary a great deal of trouble. Surely we've had enough trouble for one evening with my nephew here showing how tough he is." I flushed and glared at him, but he closed one eye in a fantastic parody of a wink which contorted the whole of one side of his face.

I danced my dance with Mary and we spent the rest of the evening in a manner that suited the lighter moments of serious people. I am afraid I got slightly drunk and told a great number of out-of-date ghost stories, most of them stolen from Monk Lewis and Una Ratcliffe, with a faint leavening of Walpole—Horace not Hugh.

CHAPTER 3

'TWAS BRILLIG

As MY UNCLE'S GUEST, I stayed at the White Lion, which suited me very well as it meant that any money I made from my reports on the Congress was sheer profit. I could not quite understand what the *Daily Courier* saw in the subject of genetics that would interest the general public, for I only could choose the subjects that interested me without any reference to the chance of their interesting others. I mentioned this to Uncle John over breakfast. He looked out from behind his *Times* and bellowed, "It's all a racket, Andrew. The *Daily Courier* fancies 'culture,' and the other penny papers fancy something else. The *Daily This* likes the idea of the Englishman as a sportsman, so their pages give prominence to any sportin' news, and the *Evening That* thinks that industry is the thing, so industrial news comes first. I like knowin' what I'll find in a paper and so I read them all. I *like* their silly childish little rackets. Of course, it's a good thing that one of the papers should be directed by culture-fanciers, or at least it seems to be good. It helps to support the scientist and the artist by popularisin' their names and misquotin' their words."

I told him about Peter's remarks to me about his blood-lust for Porter and he looked serious for a moment. Then he stuck his stubby pipe under his moustache, wiped his glasses on the sleeve of his jacket and settled them carefully askew on his nose. "Harrumph," he snorted, blowing his nose into his red bandana, "somethin'll have to be done about this. I'll have to speak to Alban about it and see if he can't give the two of them a job in London, a job where they won't need to see Porter unless they want to and I don't think there's much chance of their wantin' to see him, do you, eh?"

He levered himself out of his chair and started distributing the bundle of papers and books, which lay beside his plate, in his various pockets. The Dickson Carr detective story went into his jacket pocket, along with *The Times* and a bundle of letters. The rest of the daily papers were stowed in a poacher's pocket in the inside, a pocket that already seemed to be stuffed to bursting point.

After a fairly uneventful journey, during which the Bentley had only once showed any inclination to bicker with another road-user, a heavy steam tractor, we were more or less thrown into the centre of a group on the steps of the University. Peter was there, talking to a tall American whom he introduced as Dr. Swartz. Dr. Swartz, who was chewing an empty corn-cob pipe, shifted it with strong white teeth into the corner of his mouth and his long narrow head was broken in the middle as he smiled. "Well, Mr. Blake, I'm pleased to make your acquaintance after hearing what you did to our friend Porter last night. He once worked with me in the States—you know he comes from Canada?—and, well, I can't say we liked him very much even in those days, and from what my friend, Dr. Hatton here, tells me I guess that time has not mellowed him any."

The booming voice of my uncle broke in. "Will you children," it enquired testily, "please forget the existence of Dr. Porter for a few minutes and inform an old man, who is no doubt a bit out of date, whether this is a congress of scientists or a convocation of nursemaids, gathered together to discuss the fast behaviour of the girl at number seventeen. You should be ashamed of yourselves, and I've a good mind to treat you like naughty schoolchildren and fine you sixpence for each unnecessary mention of that man's name."

Dr. Swartz chewed nervously at his pipe and then produced a pigskin purse. "Professor, since I'm only a poor foreigner, will you take it in my national currency?" He held out a ten-cent piece, remarking to Peter and me, "I get off a penny lighter than you boys." Uncle John rumbled internally and took the coin. Then the rumbling grew to a roar and exploded into laughter. "Thank'ee, boy," he said when the laughter had again subsided to a distant roll of thunder, "you took me back more years than it's seemly for me to confess to. I suddenly saw myself sittin' on the edge of a desk and taking a tanner off a tearful small boy who had written some vulgarity on a lavatory wall. Theoretically the sixpence was to pay the cleaner for the job of deletin' the cloacal verse, but I'm afraid I forgot and embezzled it. That was the last fine I imposed until to-day and I'm goin' to embezzle once again." He slipped the dime into his waistcoat pocket and went on, "Well, then, we're agreed that from now on there'll be no unnecessary mention of the name of the quite unnecessary Doctor?"

I think we all smiled a trifle sheepishly as we gave him our promises that we would not so much as think of Porter unless we were forced to do so. I remembered that I had to find something upon which to write an article, for though I was living free and apparently holidaying, I was relying upon the money I made to live on for the next three months, while I did a little work in the British Museum on some mad nineteenth-century painters, including the cheerful Richard Dadd, who having drawn up a list of people suitable for abolition by assassination, beginning "the Pope, the King, my father," decided that the first two were impracticable and then cut his father's throat before carrying the old man down to a pond and throwing him in.

Uncle John introduced me to a stout middle-aged Indian who was an authority on the sugar-cane and who, by crossing the cane with some sort of bamboo, had managed to produce a bigger and richer cane than the native Indian one. He told me, with great joy, that most of the sugar consumed in India had formerly come from Java and that his success had so enraged the Javanese authorities that they had refused to allow him to land when he had been invited by the planters to come and advise them upon their methods.

He had the most beautiful little charts and exhibits to show how the production of native Indian sugar had increased since he had started "fiddling about with nature." An ordinary sugar-lump, marked "Twenty Years Ago," was placed beside a fancy one the size of a child's head, labelled "To-day," and a blank space had a large stencilled notice

"To-morrow?" He was a very good showman and managed to make me quite interested in the problems of agriculture in India, showing me, also, the work of other Indian plant-breeders; in particular, heads of rice the size of the tassels on a theatre drop-curtain with grains all the same size. I took a great number of notes and then decided that I would go over to the common-room and write my article on the Congress notepaper, as I had discovered that the paper upon which I had written my notes was the last I had with me.

On my way across the lawn I met Mary. "Hullo," she said, "would you like to be a guinea-pig?" I felt my ears anxiously to see if they were drooping and answered her, "Well, I haven't got a tail for you to use to pick me up and so my eyes won't drop out." She laughed, "Don't be silly, Andrew. What I meant is would you mind being used in an experiment? It's all right. Don't look so frightened, we won't hurt you. If we want to indulge in vivisection we've got to sign a certificate for each animal used, and I don't think we'd find that we'd be able to pass you on a certificate. There would be such awkward questions. No, all we want is a drop of your blood and we'll tell you your blood-group. It's always a useful thing for you to know, as you might need a transfusion sometime and it would save time then."

"If you promise not to hurt me," I replied, "I don't mind your having just one drop of my blood. What do you want to know my blood group for? What will you do with it when you've got it?" She looked at me as if to say that I would not understand and said, "Well, you know that we have a strange habit of collecting seemingly useless information in the hope that we can put it to some use later. This blood-collecting is, then, just another example of our magpie habits. It isn't really my job, but Dr. Swartz is short-handed and asked me to help. There'll be lots of other things for you to try. Come along, then."

I put on my sternest expression and reminded her that I, also, in my quiet way, was one of the world's workers and that I had an article to write, but promised that I would find Dr. Swartz's demonstration when I had finished my article, in less than an hour's time, and I said that, if they desired it, I would come disguised as a white mouse.

The information which the Indian had given me worked up into a very nice story of the "human interest" variety. I drew a picture of the Indian village with its stunted canes, no higher than a ten-year child, and that of the future, almost overshadowed by canes with flowered tassels out of the reach of a tall man. I then took the article over to the sugar exhibit and showered it to the plant-breeder, feeling that if he corrected it there would not be much fear of my making any serious mistakes. He crossed out one or two of my sentences and suggested others to take their place, and gave me several new ideas which meant that I had to go and rewrite the article. As a result of this it was nearly twelve o'clock before I reached the demonstration.

The door was open and I could see that there were only three or four people in the room. Dr. Swartz was standing beside a table on which, like musical glasses, there was a long row of small vessels half-filled with liquids. At one end of the table lay a pile of fountain-pen fillers, glass-tubes coming to a point, with a rubber bulb at the opposite end, and a heap of sheets of paper, and a box of pencils. At the other end a studious-looking young man was seated with a drawing board in front of him, on which he had pinned a large sheet of cartridge-paper divided up into sections by ruled pencil lines. Mary was filling a lot of test tubes with yellow liquid and placing them carefully in numbered stands, and another girl, also in a white overall, was writing labels which she stuck to the test tubes. It all looked terribly business-like and aseptic, reminding me of the operating theatre where I had had my appendix removed when I was a child. All my childish fears came back to me and I would have retired quietly if Mary had not turned round at that moment and cried, "Oh, there you are, Andrew, I thought you were never coming." She looked at her wrist-watch, "You said you would be here about three-quarters of an hour ago."

I explained that I had taken longer than I had intended over my article and, with unwilling feet, I advanced towards the menacing ranks of test tubes. "Sit down here," I was told and was pushed into a chair. The other girl washed the lobe of my ear with a swab of cotton-wool dipped in methylated spirit. Mary took hold of the lobe and I heard a click; she pinched my ear and said, "There, that didn't hurt, did it?" I looked round and saw that she was holding up one of her test tubes and that the yellow liquid was now pink with my blood. "How did you get that," I demanded, and she held out an instrument slightly resembling a thin hypodermic syringe. She twisted something and then held it out towards me, releasing a lever as she did so. There was a click and a tiny knife-blade shot out.

At that moment I heard steps behind me and looked round. It was Dr. Porter. He paid no attention to either Mary or me but went up to Dr. Swartz and began speaking to him in a low voice. I faced Mary and saw that she was glaring at his back as if she wished that she could stick the little knife she held in her hand through his heart. "What's the idea of the yellow stuff?" I said cheerfully. As if I had yanked her hair Mary returned to me, "Oh, that's sodium citrate. It prevents your blood coagulating. You know if you cut yourself while shaving how the blood dries into a little hard knob. The citrate prevents the sample we have taken from doing the same."

She put some of the blood on each of three microscope slides and then, with a glass rod removed a drop of liquid from various bottles and mixed it up with the blood on the slides. I heard Porter's voice raised behind me, "Then it will be all right, Swartz, if I use this place during lunch." "Quite all right, Doctor." As Porter went out of the door he met Peter coming in. Neither of them seemed to notice the other.

When Porter's footsteps had died away in the corridor, Peter jerked his thumb over his shoulder and said, "What did *he* want?" Swartz rolled his empty pipe into the corner of his mouth and replied, "He, or I suspect, Silver, has some new non-coagulant that he wants to try out. I told him he could do it during lunch."

Peter turned to Mary. "I see you've got Andrew as a victim," he remarked. "I just dropped in, Mary, to tell you that I may be a little late at lunch time. There are one or two things I must do first."

"It's all right," she replied, "I'll hang about for you outside the common-room or I'll be in the writing-room, dealing with the letters I should have written last week." Peter nodded cheerfully to me and went out. Mary continued playing tricks with my blood and then she looked up at me. "Your group is O," she said.

I had not the slightest idea what she meant, but, trying to look intelligent, I enquired "What's wrong with it? Is it very rare? Or does it mean that I've got some terrible disease which may pop up at any minute and carry me off?"

She laughed, "No, it's all correct. You are in the commonest group. We divide the blood into four groups, A, AB, B and O. A is the rarest and O is the commonest. You can give blood to any of the other groups, you're what's called a Universal Donor, but you can only receive it from another O." I wanted to know why I could not receive blood from anyone and she explained that while my blood would not clot the blood of a person in another group, their blood would form a clot in my veins and I would die. I determined that I would not have anything to do with anyone else's blood if I had any say in the matter.

Dr. Swartz beckoned me over. "Since you're here, Mr. Blake," he said, "you might as well go through the bag of tricks. Taste this and tell me whether you find it sweet or bitter."

He held out a teaspoon containing a little colourless liquid and I felt like a small boy being induced to take castor oil and I wondered faintly, remembering the way he had held out the dime to my uncle, whether he would give me a penny if I took my medicine without making a fuss. For a moment I did not taste anything, then the liquid was very sweet. I spat it out and told Dr. Swartz that I had found it anything but bitter and asked him what it was.

"Oh," he replied, "it's strange stuff, some people find it sweet and others so bitter that they can hardly keep it in their mouths. You see these," he pointed to the vessels containing liquids and I nodded. "I want you to take this teaspoon and dropper and this sheet of paper and pencil. You will see that the paper is divided up into columns headed Bitter, Sour, Brackish, Tasteless, Salt, Sweet and so on? Well, I want you to put a tick opposite the number of each of these vessels in the right column. You think you can do that?"

I answered that I thought I could, but that I hoped he hadn't laid any booby-traps for me, such as a glassful of an emetic. He assured me that he had not laid any such traps and I started off on my tasting-round. I began very carefully, tasting each drop slowly and rolling it round my tongue, but I soon decided that there were no tricks and speeded things up, making a squiggle in the appropriate column.

When I had finished the young man with the drawing-board took my paper and ran his pencil along the columns. When he reached the foot of the page he looked up at me and said, "This is very strange. You've got a very good sense of taste for you detected a point oh one solution of sea-water, but you've tasted all the sours as sweet. I've not come across that idiocrasy before this morning and then I have two cases of it." He took my name and other details and entered them on his large sheet of paper. "Can you do this?" he said, making a V out of his tongue and protruding it between his teeth. It looked very simple but I found I could not do it, though I felt that I could learn with a little practice and I said so. "Oh, no, you couldn't," he laughed, "some people can do it and others can't." I wished to know what reason he had for asking me whether I could make a V out of my tongue, but all he said was that they were just adding it to their list of things they collected. The same reason applied to the fact that the lobes of my ears were loose, a fact duly noted on its column opposite my name.

I asked Dr. Swartz if he would correct some notes for me in the afternoon, if I wrote them out before lunch, for it had occurred to me that I could make my next day's article out of the blood-grouping and tasting and thus manage to get a day ahead, which would mean that I could spend a lazy day. The lanky American said that he would be very pleased to help me and I pinched some sheets of paper from him, copied out my tastes and retired to look for a quiet corner where I could write down the various things that had happened to me, before I forgot all about them under the pressure of the new things I would see. I told Mary to tell Uncle John, if she saw him, that I had gone to do some work but would be having lunch in the common-room in about half an hour's time. "I'll tell him he'll see you in an hour," she said, "and you'll see him two hours from now. He promised to come here at eleven this morning and he has not turned up yet."

My shoes clapped noisily on the stone-paved corridors as I wandered along them in search of an unoccupied room. After I had interrupted the closing minutes of several lectures I at last found an empty laboratory and sat down, flanked on each side by the slender stems of bunsen-burners, like a fantastic devil enthroned on an altar for a black mass.

I started to write down a careful account of my treatment at the gentle hands of Mary and Dr. Swartz, but I did not seem to be able to concentrate and doodled all over the margins of my paper. When at last I had finished my notes I looked over my doodles. I have a sort of morbid interest in the products of my sub-conscious; it is rather like seeing the middle of my back or the far side of the moon. There were the usual squiggles that looked like the little red worms that I used to watch in the stagnant water-butt behind the rose-garden in my father's garden. Then there was a neat drawing of the spring lancet with which Mary had drawn the blood from my ear-lobe.

Under a black thunder-cloud I suddenly noticed the face of Dr. Porter, mounted on a broken Ionic column. I felt annoyed at the sight of his face staring out of my notes. After all, I had promised Uncle John that I would not pull up the figure of Porter unnecessarily. I felt in my trouser-pocket for a sixpence. Then I took out my pen again and obliterated the grinning face with a flood of ink.

I rolled up my notes and stuck them in my jacket pocket, thinking as I did so that Uncle John's behaviour was infectious. I did not see anyone as I walked down the corridor and out across the lawn to the common-room. The clock on the wall showed me that I had taken three-quarters of an hour to write my notes. It was nearly half-past one. I did not see Peter or Mary but, after looking around, I made out the figure of my uncle slumped in a chair. He was holding a book up with one hand, while the other held a fork which travelled in circuitous routes to and from his mouth, often taking nothing from the plate.

I made my way between the tables and sat down facing him. I had time to order my lunch and eat it and start on the coffee before he realised that I was sitting opposite him. He heaved himself up and, tearing a corner off a letter as a book-mark, closed his detective novel. "Humph, young man," he rumbled, "how long have you been here? Ten minutes, eh? Well that's not the way to treat your uncle. It doesn't show a proper respect for your elders if you don't draw their attention to the fact that they're lookin' slovenly." His eyes twinkled.

"By the way, Uncle John," I said, "I'm afraid I owe you sixpence. I doodled the face of 'that man' on the edge of my notes, and I think it's only fair that that should count as a mention, don't you?"

He put his stubby fingers together in a judicial manner and said ponderously, "Well, I think that threepence would serve in that case since you have not broadcast your doodle. Then I should fine myself for being caught in the attitude in which you found me. The fine for slovenliness has not been fixed so I suggest that we call it quits. Are you finished? Yes? Well, I wonder whether you would mind givin' me a hand with my exhibits for the next half-hour. It would help a lot if you could."

We got up and he shoved his novel into his pocket and stumped beside me towards the door. In the entrance we met Mary. She seemed to be upset about something and asked, rather sharply, "Has either of you seen Peter?" I shook my head and she brushed past us into the dining-room. Uncle John turned and looked after her over the top of his spectacles and breathed deeply.

When we were half-way across the lawn Peter ran past us, paying no attention to us. His hair was ruffled and someone seemed to have tugged at his tie. Again my uncle turned and beamed benevolently over his steel-rims.

As we entered the building we heard the clatter of running feet at the far end of the corridor. Then the figure of Professor Silver appeared, with his cockatoo plume of hair bobbing up and down as he cantered. Uncle John turned to me and boomed, "Humph, everyone seems to be in a hurry to-day."

Silver ran up to us and his voice was pitched like the screech of unoiled brakes. "Professor Stubbs, will you come and look at Ian? I think he's dead!"

CHAPTER 4

SLITHY TOVE

UNCLE JOHN polished his glasses on his sleeve and looked at Silver, who was quivering like a greyhound after a hard race, and snorted violently. Silver looked as though he was going to burst into tears and my uncle thumped him on the shoulder, a blow that nearly knocked him to his knees, grumbling, "Pull yourself together, man. Where is he? In the blood-groupin' demonstration room? Come on, Andrew."

He stumped along the corridor, his feet thumping bluntly on the stone floor, while ours merely clicked. We did not encounter anyone. The door of the demonstration room was ajar. And my uncle pushed it wider.

We paused on the threshold. Beside the tasting-table the body of Dr. Ian Porter lay spread out, his arms and legs splayed so that he looked rather like a St. Andrew's Cross, with his body as a fungoid growth at the crossing of the arms. Uncle John settled his glasses more firmly on his nose and strode into the room, his nostrils dilated like those of a race-horse. He sniffed violently and then snorted as he turned to us, "Stay where you are. I'll see to this."

Dropping on one knee beside Porter, he placed his fingers on the pulse of the right wrist, and shook his head slowly, the tangle of grey hair falling over his forehead. Then he stood up and sniffed again. He looked at the little glasses of liquid on the table and leaned over them without touching. As if someone had hit him he straightened up abruptly and turned towards us. "Come a bit nearer," he ordered, and we approached him. "That's far enough. Smell anythin'?"

The sickly smell with which all readers of detective stories are familiar hung around the neighbourhood of Porter's body. "Prussic acid?" I ventured. "Umhum," rumbled my uncle, "cyanide. Well, there's not much we can do. You, Andrew, run and ring up the police. Silver and I will keep watch to see that no one comes in here."

I ran along the corridors until I reached the janitor's cubbyhole beside the front door. It was empty but I pushed the door open and, seeing it was not a dial telephone, picked up the receiver and, when answered, asked the operator to put me through to the police. "Hullo," I said, "I am speaking from the University, where there's a Congress of Geneticists. One of the members has just been found dead in a demonstration room and there's a terrible smell of prussic acid in the room." The voice at the other end did not express the least surprise but merely replied, "I will send someone along at once. Don't let anyone go into the room. What is your name, sir? Mr. Andrew Blake. Thank you, sir."

The line went dead and I left the janitor's little office and returned

to the demonstration room. Silver stood at the door and my Uncle
John was beside Porter's body. He looked down at a sheet of paper on
the floor beside which lay a pencil with a broken point. The paper
was one of Dr. Swartz's forms with the different columns for
different tastes. It was filled in down to number 14—half-way
down. "Harrumph," snorted Uncle John, "the poor devil was
amusin' himself by tastin' but he hadn't time to write down the
taste of number 15, for, if I'm not mistaken, it's a glassful of
cyanide. It's funny, though. I wonder why he didn't smell it. I'm
sure I'd have thought there was something wrong if I'd smelled
that. But then, of course, I use the stuff for sprayin' fruit trees and
I'm also a reader of detective stories."

He seemed to be talking to himself. I delivered my message
about allowing no one into the room and he moved towards the
door. He took his short pipe out of one pocket and a piece of thick
brown twist and a penknife out of the other. He appeared to be
thinking deeply as he stuck the empty pipe in his mouth and
shredded the tobacco into the palm of his hand. He clicked the
knife shut and rubbed the brown curls between his palms. Taking
the pipe from his mouth he tilted the tobacco into it, cleaning out
the crevices between the fingers of his left hand with his right
forefinger. He lighted his pipe and sucked strongly. He did not say
anything. I knew that he was wondering whether this was going to
be a difficult murder to solve and whether he could solve it. He was
already seeing himself as the great detective.

All this time Silver had said nothing, but had remained at the door
trembling. Suddenly he started to speak quickly, and his voice was
like the sound of nutmegs being grated. "I left him here at a
quarter-past one and went down to my hotel to get some notes for my
paper this afternoon. When I got back I found him lying there, like
that, dead." He ran a finger round inside his collar. "It's very hot in
here, isn't it?" He suddenly put his hand up to his forehead and
started to sob violently, a dry metallic throbbing.

Uncle John took out his watch, an enormous silver turnip that
nearly filled the palm of his hand. "It's just three minutes to two
now," he observed, paying no attention to Silver, "and we left the
common-room at about eighteen minutes to. Well, say it took the
same time for us to get over here as it took for Silver to examine
Porter, it would seem that he found him somewhere about twenty to
two."

There were steps in the corridor and we turned to see the janitor
approaching, followed by about half a dozen men. His face was

shocked as he said, "Is one of you gentlemen Mr. Blake? Did you ring
up for the police?" I assured him that I had indeed telephoned the
police and his face cleared a little; anything, I could see, was better
than that he should be the victim of a practical joker.

A youngish man, in a neat grey suit, came forward. "Mr. Blake," he
asked and again I admitted my identity, "I'm Inspector Hargrave. I got
your message and came straight up. Would you introduce me to these
gentlemen, please?" I introduced my uncle and Professor Silver.

The inspector acknowledged the introductions politely and then
went on into the demonstration room, followed by his men, who
carried their truck and gear in large leather cases. The inspector
looked at Porter's body and then at the glasses on the table. Just as my
uncle had done he jerked back when his head came above number
fifteen. His men were setting up cameras on tripods and looking
round the room. The inspector looked at his watch and then towards
the door.

At that moment the janitor came down the passage followed by a
little man in a black suit carrying a black bag. Carefully averting his
eyes from the body on the floor, the janitor looked straight at Inspector Hargrave and announced, in a voice as hollow as an echo, "Dr.
Flanagan for you, Inspector." The little doctor pushed past us, his eyes
fixed on the corpse, but my Uncle John reached out and grabbed his
shoulder, swinging him round, and boomed, "Well, Joe Flanagan,
you're lookin' well."

The doctor stared at him and exclaimed, "John Stubbs, by all that's
wonderful. It must be twenty years since I saw you and I didn't expect
to find you mixed up in sudden death. I thought that your line was
vegetable, slow growing and slow dying." He laughed and his laughter
sounded as though someone had pulled out the wrong stop on a
church organ. Silver shuddered at the sound of the laughter and the
doctor looked at him and straightened his face, remarking, "Once I've
finished with this business, John, we must have a drink together for
old times' sake."

He bustled over to the body and looked up at Inspector Hargrave,
who said, "It's all right, Doctor, you can go ahead. We've finished for
the present." The doctor bent down and rolled Porter over, revealing a
broken dropper under his neck and a teaspoon. One of the policemen
shovelled the fragments upon a piece of paper and laid them on the
table. The doctor bent over and put his nose towards Porter's mouth.
"Ach," he said, and straightened his head; he lifted the eyelids and
looked at the eyes closely.

At that moment there was a disturbance in the passage. The

noise-makers were Dr. Swartz, Mary and Peter, and the young man and girl whose names I did not know. "Well, well, and what's the matter here," said Dr. Swartz, and then he saw the body, twisted about like a half-filled sack of potatoes. He removed his corn-cob and whistled slowly between his teeth, "So he's got it at last. Well, he's been asking for it the last fifteen years to my certain knowledge."

I noticed that the inspector was listening intently and trod heavily on the lank American's foot. He put his pipe back in his mouth and rolled it to one side. "I suppose this means that my demonstration is off for to-day," he observed ruefully. "Well, that's a dam' nuisance."

Neither Mary nor Peter had said anything. Peter looked at me and said, "Well, this is none of my business so I suppose I'll be getting along." The inspector interrupted him, "Just a moment, sir, if you please. I'm afraid I'll need to ask you all a few questions first. Jenkins," he turned to one of his men, "just run along and ask the janitor if I can have the use of two unoccupied rooms."

We stood in silence until the detective reappeared, followed slowly by the janitor. The inspector spoke to him in an undertone and then turned to us, "Will you ladies and gentlemen please follow me? I'm sorry to disturb you like this, but I have my duty to do, you know."

Like one of those crocodiles in which schoolgirls enjoy their ration of fresh air, we followed him. First came my uncle and Professor Silver, then Dr. Swartz and myself, his assistants, and Mary and Peter. One of the detectives walked at the tail of this procession, as if to see that none of us evaporated on the journey.

The janitor inserted a Yale-key into a lock and opened a door. We found ourselves in another corridor, with a large room at the far end, an office on the left-hand side and a laboratory on the right. These were the Director of Chemistry's private offices. Inspector Hargrave looked into the large room and then into the office. "Well," he said, "I think you'd better wait here and I'll go into the office and Detective Jenkins will tell you when I want you." He looked at us and asked, "Which of you gentlemen was it found the body?"

The shivering Silver quaked a little more to indicate that he was the discoverer of the unpleasant treasure-trove. The inspector looked at him sympathetically, saying, "Will you come with me, sir? You look as though this had been a shock. Would you like a drink?"

Silver nodded his head weakly and his lock of hair bobbed slowly up and down. Inspector Hargrave nodded to the man who had brought up the tail of our procession and he disappeared, returning in a few minutes with a glass half-full of brandy and water, which he handed to Silver, who drank it off straight.

We were alone in the room but the detective, Jenkins, stood at the door, silent as a ghost but just as effective in preventing conversation about the subject which was uppermost in all our minds. My Uncle John, like a shaggy old Highland bull, lumbered about the room, pulling books out of the shelves, flipping the pages over in an absent-minded way and then replacing them. As he usually replaced them upside down I followed him slowly and corrected this.

No one said anything and it was a relief when we heard Inspector Hargrave call to Jenkins, "Please ask Professor Stubbs to come along now."

My uncle ruffled his hair, put another match to his pipe, and left the room surrounded by clouds of smoke, leaving me with the impression that I had just seen Elijah wafted up to heaven and that I, the earnest disciple, was waiting for his cloak to fall upon my shoulders.

Mary and Peter were whispering in a corner and the young man and the girl were seated one at each end of the couch, in strict propriety, with their eyes fixed straight ahead of each of them. Dr. Swartz seemed to be engaged in some mathematical problem, for he was covering the backs of envelopes with small neat figures and then crossing them out, while his empty corn-cob rose and fell between his eyes and his chin, metronomic in its regularity.

Occupying the bottom row of one of the bookcases I saw a morocco-bound set of the *Encyclopaedia Britannica*. I went across and took out the volume containing cyanide. Unfortunately I could not understand that and, as there was a cross reference to prussic acid, I exchanged the volumes. This article was very nearly as obscure from my point of view, but I managed to extract from it the information that prussic acid was a highly volatile liquid, an extremely fast poison and one that was very simply prepared. I thought that, if the materials had been in the various bottles which I saw in the lab. When I had written up my notes, I would have been able to make it myself. The instructions appeared to be simple enough for a child; even one less intelligent than Macaulay's proverbial schoolboy.

I was digesting this entrancing information which I had just began to swallow when Jenkins popped his head into the room. "Will you come this way, Mr. Blake, please?" I put the *Encyclopaedia* carefully back into its place and followed the detective. There was a hollow feeling in my stomach which reminded me horribly of walking along a passage to the headmaster's study, knowing that I would receive first an unpleasant lecture and then a beating.

Inspector Hargrave was seated behind a desk, with his back to the window. He motioned me to a chair opposite. At one end of the desk, looking very cramped, a young detective sat entrenched behind a reporter's notebook.

"Mr. Blake," the inspector said, "I am sorry to have inconvenienced you in this way, but you must understand that it is my duty to investigate the circumstances of Dr. Porter's death. I gather from your uncle, Professor Stubbs, that you are not a scientist, and I think I would probably find it useful if you could give me your impressions of the late Dr. Porter and also any facts that you know about his death. That is, I would like you to tell me when you last saw him alive and any other details you can remember."

I told him that I did not know Porter well, having only met him the previous day, but that I had not felt attracted by what I had seen of him. I was congratulating myself upon my skill in avoiding any mention of the dance when Inspector Hargrave held up his hand. "Just a moment, Mr. Blake," he said smoothly, "just a moment. I understand that you had a—well, let's call it a disagreement, with Dr. Porter last night. Is that correct?"

"No," I replied firmly, determined that I was not going to get mixed up in any murder if I could help it. "What happened was that Dr. Porter, who was extremely drunk, was fooling about and I tapped him playfully and he passed-out."

The inspector nodded wisely, but I felt that he did not believe me. "Go on, Mr. Blake," he urged gently, "tell me what you know of the events of this morning."

Feeling that it would not improve my situation if I slurred over anything else, I gave him as full an account of the morning as I could manage, including all sorts of details which had nothing to do with my actions, hoping vaguely that I was boring him as a recompense for his unbelieving look. When I mentioned Porter's visit to the blood-grouping room he again held up his hand. "Half a minute, Mr. Blake, who was present in the room when Dr. Porter announced his intention of working there at lunch-time?"

I thought for a moment and replied, "Dr. Swartz, his two assistants, Dr. Hatton, Miss Lewis and myself." He looked across to the short-hand writer and said, "Got that?" The writer nodded briskly and held his pencil poised ready to take down the next thing I said.

The rest of my story did not take long. I said nothing about Peter's flurried look when we had encountered him running after Mary, thinking that he probably would prefer to give his own account of how he had spent the morning and that there was no point in sowing unnecessary suspicion in Inspector Hargrave's too receptive mind.

I thought I had finished, when the inspector beckoned with his hand, a gesture to me to remain seated. "I suppose, Mr. Blake," he said, "it's just a matter of form—but you have someone who can vouch for the fact that you were in the deserted laboratory from about a quarter to one until half-past?"

"Of course not," I retorted, irritated, "haven't I just said that I went there in order to be *alone*. I don't call it being *alone* if I take along half a dozen witnesses to vouch for my actions." The inspector smiled. "That's all right," he said, "I just have to ask. I have to work to a routine and if I don't ask questions like that those higher up come down on me like a load of bricks for writing incomplete reports. I think that is all I want from you at present. Thank you very much, Mr. Blake, you have been very long-suffering."

I felt that I had perhaps spoken a trifle rudely so I did my best to look apologetic, and murmured something about being only too pleased if I had been of any use. Inspector Hargrave smiled and said, "That is very kind of you. I wonder whether you could go to the demonstration room and get one of my men and show him the laboratory where you sat to write out your notes? Thank you."

Outside in the corridors there were one or two small groups hanging about, and I heard the name Porter mentioned once or twice as I brushed past them, ignoring the curious glances that were cast at me. I remembered, with a wistful vagueness that, in spite of flood, battle and sudden death, I was a journalist. So I phoned the local office of the rag and gave them as much of the low-down as I could, considering that I knew nothing low about the case and was as far from a showdown as the inspector.

A uniformed policeman stood outside the door of the demonstration room. I told him that I had a message from Inspector Hargrave. He opened the door a couple of inches, standing in front of the crack so that I could not see inside, and said hoarsely, "Message from the inspector." A stout sergeant, in a shiny blue serge suit, came out and I told him that Inspector Hargrave had asked me to take him along to the lab. to show him where I had been working.

Swinging his arms in a military manner, the sergeant followed me along the corridors until we arrived at the door of the lab. I threw open the door and walked over to the place where I had seated myself that morning, flanked by the bunsen-burners. I looked round the room and thought that I had not realised its size during the time I had been working there. At the far end of the room, beside a white porcelain sink, there was a mass of glass tubing and retorts and several wide-mouthed bottles with glass stoppers, and tall ones with narrow necks.

The sergeant took out a thick black note-book and pencil, wetting it between his lips, and started to draw a very careful plan of the room. While he was doing this I wandered off down the room, admiring the jars full of powders and crystals of all the colours of the rainbow and several that the sky had not thought of, and the elaborate tangles of glass-tubing which looked as though they had originated in the brain of Heath Robinson, with a little assistance from the early H. G. Wells.

At length I arrived at the sink and looked at the apparatus which had been set up there. I wondered what sort of experiment it had been and looked idly at the bottles behind the glassware. I had never before believed that people could "nearly drop down dead from shock," but I felt as though I could. The bottles were labelled plainly, in large red and black letters, DISTILLED WATER, SULPHURIC ACID and PRUSSIATE OF POTASH. My few minutes' browsing in the *Encyclopaedia Britannica* came back at me like a boomerang. I hoped that I was wrong, but I did not feel that there was much doubt that someone had been having a shot at making prussic acid.

It occurred to me that, if I mentioned my discovery to the sergeant, there was very little doubt that he would jump to the unfortunate conclusion that I had been starting a private cyanide brewery. I did not want this to happen so I wandered back to him, looking as nonchalant as possible, to see how his labours of map-making were progressing. He wet his pencil after every stroke and in the middle of each he would pause, bite a chip off the blunt end, close one eye and lean back, looking reflectively at his handiwork. I leaned up against the bench to hide the fact that my knees were showing a slight inclination to knock together.

"Well," I said cheerfully in a voice that sounded as though it was a couple of miles from my mouth, "how's the job going, Sergeant? Nearly finished it? I'm beginning to feel that I could do with a cup of tea." He looked up at me and blew out his cheeks. "I am finished, sir. Will you just put a cross where you sat?" I put my mark, thinking that the sergeant had succeeded in wasting ten minutes. We went out together and he moved the key from the inside of the door to the outside and locked it, putting the key away in his pocket.

I went over to the common-room where I found my uncle seated alone at a table with a large pot of tea in front of him, blowing ferociously through his whiskers to frighten off the people who were obviously dying to ask him questions. He reminded me of one of those eighteenth-century prints of bull-baiting, with the hoary old bull presenting its lowered head to the snarling snapping terriers. When he saw me he bellowed, "Come over here, Andrew, where we can be

uninterrupted by chitter-chatter!" This rebuke seemed to have its
desired effect, for the gaping heads quickly were turned towards
anchovy-toast and cakes. I tried his technique of snorting to avoid
conversational openings and managed to get across the room without
anyone having spoken to me.

"I had to send Silver off home," my uncle rumbled. "He looks as
though someone had kicked him in the pit of the stomach. I knew he
was very attached to Porter, but I didn't realise that it went as deep as
all that. For about half an hour I had him here, throbbin' like a
turbine-engine, and I was afraid he was goin' to go off his head, so I
filled him up with whisky and put him in a taxi. I expect he'll have got
over it by to-morrow morning; he'll have such a hangover that he won't
be able to think of Porter." He looked at me and growled, "Now I
think of it you're a bit green yourself. What's the matter. You haven't
been meeting the late Doctor's ghost, have you? I wouldn't be
surprised if he walked a bit." He spoke with relish. "He'll have a good
deal to receive in the way of forgiveness before he'll be allowed to
enter heaven."

I said, quietly in case anyone was eavesdropping, "There are several
things I want to speak to you about, but I can't do it here. I know
where the poison came from." He did not move but contented himself
with grunting. I poured myself a cup of tea, nearly as black as Indian
ink and so strong that I quite expected to see it burst the pot asunder.

We drank our tea in silence, broken only by the whine and wheeze
of Uncle John's pipe. When I had finished he hoisted himself out of
his chair, mumbling, "I think we'll go back to the White Lion. No one
can interrupt us there, and you can give me a full list of your
indiscretions, and misstatements, for I've no doubt but that you have
been tyin' yourself up in a net under the impression that you were
makin' things sound better."

The Bentley seemed almost to drive itself, or, at least, I am sure
that my uncle drove very nearly automatically. He seemed to be
thinking and was quite unperturbed when we slid away from the sides
of tramcars or cut into the three or four feet separating two cyclists.
He shot, unobserved, past several sets of traffic lights whose red eyes
winked furiously and drew up, to the accompaniment of vigorous
hooting from behind, for a green light to change to red before he
proceeded. Without any pretence at nonchalance I sat beside him and
prayed, quite sincerely, that the next corner might disclose an uninhabited
stretch of road. My prayers were unanswered. Each stretch was fuller
of hair-breadth escape than the last. When we drew up outside the

hotel I was not surprised to feel that my collar was a damp and clammy pillory round my neck.

Uncle John stumped into the bar, booming for beer. We sat down in a corner and once the pint mugs had been replenished, he rumbled at me, "Come on, now, tell me your story. And don't miss anything out. Begin where I left you with Peter and Swartz this mornin', and go right up to tea-time. Tell me everythin'."

CHAPTER 5

GIMBLING IN THE WABE

"WELL NOW YOU'VE HEARD how Andrew here has messed things up I'd like to hear the stories you others have to tell."

The voice of my uncle echoed enormously in the small private room where we were seated round a table covered with the debris of a gargantuan meal, built on the same lines as Uncle John. Mary and Peter did not appear to have quite recovered from the afternoon. They were still jumpy and showed an inclination to look into the corners of the room whenever there was a slight sound. As a concession to the occasion Dr. Swartz had replaced his unused corn-cob with a long thin unlighted cigar, which he was engaged in slowly eating as he rolled it from one corner of his mouth to the other. Occasionally he removed it from his mouth and, holding it between his finger and thumb, crackled it beside his ear and then, apparently satisfied, returned it to his teeth where the slow mastication continued.

My uncle roared and a waiter, who looked slightly frightened, appeared. He was ordered to bring a keg of brandy, or better still two kegs of brandy and several gallons of coffee. When this order had been transferred into the everyday language of the hotel and the waiter appeared with two bottles and a vast coffee pot, which looked as though it was an hotel heirloom, Uncle John beamed benevolently at him and roared, "That'll have to do, I suppose. Now if I want anythin' else I'll ring for it. We don't want to be disturbed."

When the brandy had been distributed in bubble-glasses, chosen not for their original purpose but on account of their size, Uncle John turned to Dr. Swartz, "Now then, as it was your demonstration that was graced by the presence of Ian Porter's departure for a place where he will be welcomed, I think I should start with you. Will you tell me everything that you did this morning. I'm not a policeman but as an avid reader of detective stories I don't want anyone to be wrongly suspected if I can help it. Don't be afraid to tell me anythin' you like. I don't mind if one of you *did* murder Porter, but if you did I hope you managed it in such a way that you won't be found out. Anyhow, just treat my wish as the wish of an old man who has to be humoured." Dr. Swartz took a drink of brandy and a new cigar and, leaning back in his chair, started. "Well, I won't bother you with my breakfast and journey up to the University. Once I got there I went on arranging my demonstration which I started work on yesterday. I laid out the taste-testing material, measuring a little out of each of my bottles into the glasses. My assistants came in as I finished doing this and I was at work putting a label on to each vessel when Mary here arrived. I had asked her if she would give me a hand as Miss Dorn, my usual assistant in blood-grouping, was knocked down by a bus in London and I was, in consequence, shorthanded. She did the taste-test out of curiosity and then several people came in to be grouped and to fill up the taste-test forms. Let me think," he bit a piece off his cigar and took another sip of brandy, "there were, Von Friedlander, from the Kaiser Wilhelm Institut in Berlin, with him was Kobofsky; after that I had Powys, Cortot and then Silver."

My uncle held up a hand like a policeman and his questions rumbled in his throat like distant thunder, "What time would this be?"

The American chewed at his cigar. "About ten forty-five or so. I wasn't timing anything so I had no reason to look at either my watch or the clock."

"Was he alone or had he Porter with him? What made him come? Had you asked him specially?"

With the air of one arranging a bundle of straws in order of their respective lengths, Swartz did some thinking. "Well, I had made no secret of the fact that I was doing my stuff as I wanted as many people as possible to come along and Silver was talking to Von Friedlander when I asked him to come along during the morning and I suppose he thought, as I meant him to, that he was included in the invitation. The reason for asking them along during the morning is that most demonstrations are slack until after lunch, when they are overworked. No, he hadn't Porter with him, though he said that he would be along later. There was no reason for Porter to come. You know he worked with me in the States for some time and he knows all about the taste-testing. He and I used to do it nearly every day, just to see if our tastes altered at all. He had a much better sense of taste than I have and showed practically no variation from day to day."

My Uncle John grunted, something seemed to be worrying him, but all he said was, "He must have been seein' if it had varied at all after a longish time. They found a paper half-filled in beside his body. It's funny, though, if his taste was as good as all that, that he took a sip of cyanide without noticin' it." He shook himself like a spaniel after a swim. "Never mind, though, just go on with your story." In spite of a few half-hearted protests he filled up the brandy glasses and then, after polishing them on the bottom of his waistcoat, settled his steel-rimmed glasses firmly on his nose and beamed round the table, like a cross between a jovial Dickens' character and a more or less clean-shaven Santa Claus.

"There's not very much more. I had one or two students in for the bag of tricks and then Andrew Blake came in, looking rather frightened as if he was afraid that we would kill him. While he was there Porter came in, to ask if he could use the room during lunch for some experiment with a new non-coagulant he's been working on. I couldn't see any reason for refusing his request so I told him I didn't mind so long as he did not mess up the demonstration. The suggestion that he might interfere with my things stung him a bit, I think. After that I put Blake through the show and then tidied up a bit. When I left—at what time? Oh I suppose about five past one. When I left my assistants had just gone and Mary was tidying up the blood-grouping materials. I then, not feeling very hungry, walked down to Powys' exhibit. I wanted to see his cross-bred dogs. He was there and I had lunch with him in an inn called *The Seven Stars*. You know it? Yes. Well, after lunch, a fairly quick one, I went back to the University, leaving Powys with his dogs. I met the others in the corridor and you know the rest."

Uncle John opened his eyes and chuckled, "So you've got a pretty fair alibi, son, eh? I think that's fairly simple. Now, on the principle of ladies first, you tell us your story, Mary."

I will not bother to write down the whole of Mary's account of how she spent her morning as the greater part of it was merely a duplication of the things we had already been told by Dr. Swartz. When she arrived at the departure of Swartz for lunch she hesitated and, after a quick sip at her almost untouched brandy, said, "Well then I met Peter and I think that's all."

My uncle looked at her over the top of his spectacles in a benevolent way, "Come, come, my dear," he grumbled gently, "I want your version of what you did as well as Peter's. No, no, don't be silly. I'm not tryin' to trap you. It's only that I'd like to have your version as well as his, in case he misses anything that you noticed." Mary had looked at him sharply, but as he spoke so gently she eased back in her chair.

"All right," she said slowly. "After Dr. Swartz left the room I cleaned up the blood-testing things and laid them ready for the afternoon. I suppose that took me another three or four minutes. Then I went out into the corridor where I met Peter. He asked me if, before lunch, I would read through his paper as there were one or two points of which he was doubtful. We went in search of somewhere quiet and sat down in the room where the rat and mouse people have their exhibits, beside Cortot's new travelling cage."

She was interrupted by my uncle tapping on the table with the edge of his hand. "I'm sorry to interrupt you, my dear, but I just wondered what you thought of the cage." His eyes twinkled disarmingly. Mary looked puzzled. "I didn't look at it very closely but I thought it seemed a bit too elaborate, and I couldn't see very many advantages from it, except on the grounds of neatness." My uncle nodded wisely and said, "That's all right. Will you please go on now?"

"I read Peter's paper and thought it was pretty good. Peter wanted to wash his hands as he had been mucking about all morning and so I went on alone to the common-room. I met you, you remember, just coming out." My uncle nodded again and turned to Peter. "Well, sir, I think she's told you everything. I washed my hands and ran across after her." "Humph. Did either of you see anyone between the time you left the demonstration room and the time you went over to the common-room for lunch?"

Peter lit a cigarette and looked thoughtful. "No, I don't think I saw anyone. Unless, just wait a moment . . . I have a faint idea I saw Silver going along towards the demonstration room as I left the lavatory to run after Mary. If I did see him I suppose it was just about the time when he went along and found the body of that swine."

He looked around the table pugnaciously as if seeking our reaction to his disregard of the *de mortuis nihil nisi bonum* taboo, but if he hoped for some contradiction it did not come. Uncle John wagged his shaggy head like an amiable dog. "Harrumph," he snorted, "well we don't seem to be much further on, do we? As far as can be seen the demonstration room was empty from about ten past one." He drew a bundle of papers out of his pocket and, selecting an envelope not already covered with notes, started to scribble upon it with his fat fountain pen. "Until, say, twenty to two when Silver entered it and stumbled upon the body of Porter." He wrote several names down the page and said, his voice suddenly booming like that of a faulty wireless, "Now, then, I'll make a list of everyone that we know about at present, just to see who had the opportunity, motive and so on to murder Porter. I'll put myself at the top of the list so that no one can say that I'm being unfair. This business of making a list is common to many of the best detective stories, so I don't see why we should not follow their examples, do you?" No one said anything to show disapproval, so he started scribbling, in his small neat handwriting. The writing spread over the backs of several envelopes before he leaned back in his seat, beaming happily. "Now, lady and gentlemen," he said, wagging the papers at us, "I'm going to pass these notes of mine round and I don't want anyone to say anythin' until I have them back, when I will receive all complaints, congratulations and corrections with gratitude."

The papers ran as follows:

JOHN STUBBS. *Motive:* general dislike. *Opportunity:* not, at the moment, visible. *Remarks:* has been heard by Andrew Blake to state that it would not be a bad thing if Porter were to be murdered and also said that he hoped no one fumbled the job as if necessary he could manage it very cleverly. Motive is rather weak but as murders have been committed for a few shillings before now that need not matter. *Principal objection:* appears to have alibi; lunching in view of many people in common-room, and is not the size of person who would escape notice slipping in and out of room.

ANDREW BLAKE. *Motive:* dislike and a desire to fight other's battles for them. *Opportunity:* shut up alone in laboratory in which there are the materials and apparatus for the production of prussic acid, which, also, he appears to know how to prepare. Unsupported statement that he only discovered method from *Encyclopaedia* this afternoon. Motive is weak but fact of fight last night shows willingness to use force; however, method employed is not that of man who will deal out blows.

MAXWELL SILVER. *Motive:* perhaps annoyance at Porter's thieving. *Opportunity:* unknown (to be looked into). *Remarks:* unlikely, as he was Porter's one really intimate friend. Probably possesses technical ability required in the preparation of cyanide.

HERMAN SWARTZ. *Motive:* dislike, or unknown. *Opportunity:* nil, according to his alibi. *Remarks:* seems to be impossible.

PETER HATTON. *Motive:* jealousy, and intense dislike. *Opportunity:* only in conjunction with Mary Lewis (*see below*). *Remarks:* method does not seem to be one that would be favoured by Hatton. If P. had been killed by violence there would have been strong reason to suspect him.

MARY LEWIS. *Motive:* hatred and anger at P.'s behaviour. *Opportunity:* see Hatton *above. Remarks:* "poisoning is a woman's crime." This statement is not true; percentage of women poisoners over men admitted but all the same method one used by large number of men.

X. *Motive:* unknown. *Opportunity:* unknown. *Remarks:* it is impossible to make remarks on an unknown quantity—except for the sake of making the remarks.

When the paper had gone round the table my uncle looked at us over the top of his glasses and beamed in a friendly way. "Hey," he boomed and the frightened-looking waiter popped his head in at the door. "Beer in tankards." When the beer had arrived and we were drinking it slowly, he looked up from the list and mumbled, "Well, I don't know what you think, but for the present I'd like to keep our friend X out of it. He's such a strange chap, and he only appears in the worst detective stories when the author cannot think of a way in which to link up one of the suspects with the murder, havin' provided him with too good an alibi. So we come to the unpleasant fact that it would seem that one of us here, or Professor Silver, committed the murder, or, at least, we've got to prove that none of the people on this list could possibly have killed Porter. I'm sorry to be so blunt but it's an unpleasant fact and we must face it, for you'll find that the police will presumably come to the same conclusion. Of course, it would be pleasant if we could find an X or if, say, Silver during a brainstorm had decided to murder his best friend. But, an' it's a big but, this murder was fairly carefully planned."

He leaned back and took a pull at his tankard. "I don't, myself, see Silver indulgin' in murder as one of his side-lines, but then I'm only an amateur at this game, so that I wouldn't know as much about it as the police and they may have chosen Silver as suspect. What does anyone think about Silver as murderer?"

No one spoke and he continued, "Well, we seem agreed that Porter's murderer was not Silver. Now Swartz, have you anythin' to say to my notes on you? Heh?" The lanky American stretched himself and chewed a careful ring round a new cigar. He did not look at my uncle but fixed his eyes on his empty brandy glass. I had the impression that he was under some strain as he spoke, though his tone was light enough. "Well, I guess you're all washed-up about motive, Professor, for you see—" He paused and I noticed that his teeth went nearly right through the cigar. "I have a stronger motive than any of you. There was once a girl . . . it's a longish time ago now, that's why I can speak about it without feeling . . . she had nothing much to do with me . . . but I hoped that one day she would be Mrs. Swartz." He laughed dryly, the laugh of a lecturer making an academic joke. "Well, Porter was my assistant. He came to the States from McGill. He left me suddenly to go to England and I was glad to see him go, for I had never liked him much." He laughed again and there were little drops of sweat at the wrinkled corners of his eyes. "The girl, you see, wasn't so glad when he left and she looked down the wrong end of an automatic. One of those toys that college students have—to make them feel tough—but it was big enough for its purpose. . . . She was pregnant . . . of course, I couldn't have proved anything but I had no doubt that Porter didn't want to be saddled with a wife and child at that stage of his career . . . he was ambitious, as you all know . . . he once told me his motto . . . 'He travels farthest who travels alone.'"

Again he paused and reached out for the brandy bottle. When he laid down the glass he seemed to be quite himself again. "I think that's all, Professor, but you see I had a motive and I can't say I'm sorry he's dead. I'd have liked to have done it myself and I hope that whoever it was gets away with it, just so long as no one else suffers from his deed." I thought he had finished, but he started again. "And, as regards your lack of opportunity, there again I have a loophole. Powys left me alone for a few minutes with his dogs, I'd forgotten that, while he went to get some food for them, and I could easy enough have gotten across to my room and back in the time."

My uncle grunted and looked at him in a kindly way. "Thank you for your frankness," he rumbled. "That makes things a great deal clearer. Now, has anyone else got anything to add to the statements they gave me? Andrew?" He looked at me and I shook my head. "Peter and Mary?" His glance was sharp but he accepted their statements that they had nothing to say without comment. "Humph, then, as I'm an old man I think I will break up this party and go to my bed, and if any of you remember anythin' that's slipped your memories I'll be glad to hear it in the mornin'."

When he had said his varying good-nights he turned to me. "Look here, my boy, are you tired after all the excitement of the day? No? Well, come along to my room and we'll have a talk about things. I'd like to write down all that we've heard to-night and try to make sense out of it. There's a lot of it doesn't make sense. For instance, there are too many motives and too many people who would have been glad to kill Porter, even without the mysterious Mr. X."

He picked up the telephone in his room and demanded a number from the operator. "Hullo, Joe," he boomed a moment later, "how did you get on? No what? Hmm, that's strange. Were there any signs of an injection? No? Hmm, then it's cleverer than I thought. The gums? No? What, Joe? Of course, I'm playing the detective. I've waited for this opportunity for a long time and now I've got it I'm going to make sure they don't hang the wrong person. Still the same person, am I? Huff?" He slammed down the microphone and blew out his cheeks furiously. "Man doesn't know what he's talking about—says I'm a sort of G. K. Chesterton who still believes in romance and chivalry. Wouldn't be surprised if I carried a sword-stick in order to rescue any damsels in distress I chanced to encounter. Shows he's a fool." He puffed fiercely and glowered at me, demanding, "He's wrong, ain't he?"

"No, I think he's probably right," I replied, and he laughed so loud that I quite expected a messenger to appear from the manager to request him to make less noise. His glasses nearly fell off his blunt nose and his tangled grey hair fell into his eyes. "All right, all right," he bellowed, "I'm a Dumas figure, the hero of a cloak and sword novelette. I don't mind. That was the police-surgeon, Joe Flanagan, and he's puzzled, dam' puzzled. Can't find any traces of cyanide in Porter's guts and don't believe that he drank it out of the glass, and the police say there are neither lip-marks nor fingerprints on the glass. Joe doesn't think that Porter would have sniffed strongly enough at the cyanide to asphyxiate himself and suggests that he was injected with the stuff. But, and here's the snag, he can't find any punctures anywhere on the person of the late Doctor Porter. Says he went over the body very carefully. Must have been like searchin' the Matterhorn for a snowball."

He grunted once or twice and then scraped out and filled his pipe. "Harruph," he snorted, "I want to relax. And I relax best when I'm reading. Would you mind, Andrew, getting me my Shakespeare from the car? I want to look up somethin'." I found the volume sandwiched between a detective story and Morgan's *Genetics of Drosophila* and took it back to him. He had not moved since I had left the room and the clouds of smoke from his pipe gave me the impression of a vast geni, raised from some magical brass bottle.

He took the book from me and nodded his head towards the desk in the window. "Sit down and try to write out everythin' that we have heard to-night. Whether it has any bearin' on Porter's death or not. Don't miss anythin' if you can help it. We have heard some quite interestin' things, quite interestin'."

As I wrote I heard him mumbling away to himself. It must have been nearly two o'clock when I drew a line at the bottom of my fifteenth sheet of hotel notepaper. My uncle was lying back in his chair with his eyes closed and the smoke from his pipe hung in light drifts about the egg-and-dart pattern of the cornice of the ceiling. The Shakespeare lay open on his lap. Without opening his eyes he grumbled, "Finished, Andrew? Then leave the papers and buzz off to bed now. I think I know how Porter was murdered but it doesn't bring us much further towards the solution of why or who."

I demanded that he should tell me the method but he chuckled gustily. "No, no, let an old man sleep on his secret. All right, I'll give you a hint. The answer to how is in the Shakespeare on my lap. And then it was only mock-murder. Good night."

His good-night was decisive and I saw that my curiosity would not be satisfied until he wished to satisfy it. I was too tired to try and work out the clue he had given me and all I could remember of Shake-speare was "To-morrow and to-morrow and to-morrow..."

CHAPTER 6

HE BURBLED

"Thoughts black, hands apt, drugs fit, and time agreeing:
Confederate season, else, no creature seeing:
Thou mixture rank, of midnight weeds collected,
With Hecat's ban, thrice blasted, thrice infected,
Thy natural magic, and dire property,
On wholesome life, usurp immediately."

MY UNCLE'S VOICE thundered down the dining room and his face looked serious. "I can't tell you why, Andrew, but I don't like it. I don't like it at all. Maybe I'm frightened by false fire, but the only explanation I can see is devilish."

I had only just taken my seat at the breakfast table, having overslept as a result of my labours so late the previous night, and for a moment I was puzzled, being unused to having *Hamlet* roared at me over the bacon and eggs. Then I understood, but I was still bewildered as to the meaning or reason for pouring poison into Porter's ear.

"Porter wouldn't be lying asleep waiting for someone to kill him," I said, "so I don't see quite what you mean."

Uncle John ran his blunt fingers through his mop of grey hair, tangling the work of his hairbrush. "I don't exactly know what I mean myself. But if what I think is right then it's pretty devilish—too devilish for my liking—and it may mean that I've got to find Mr. X after all. On the other hand," he grinned benignly, "it means that the ranks of possible Mr. X's have been thinned down to the ranks of Porter's associates, those whom he knew well enough to ask to help him with whatever he was up to. I must go now and phone Joe Flanagan to find out if I'm right and I hope I'm not."

His heavy figure lumbered between the fragile tables. I watched him go and, spreading a fragment of toast with Oxford marmalade, wondered vaguely whether it was possible to poison anyone by pouring poison into the ear, and anyhow how one was to set about a job like that. It would mean that Porter would need to be drugged first and even then it seemed a waste of time to first drug him and then to poison him in a roundabout manner. Why not just poison him right away and have done with it? I tried to think of a method of making him drink cyanide before he had time to taste it or smell it. Suppose, for instance, someone jovial had challenged him to race round the tasting and had set the pace, how would that do? It would not do at all. I remembered the smashed dropper lying under Porter's body and also Dr. Flanagan's statement that however else he had died he had not died from drinking the cyanide. I took out a pencil and started to scribble on the margin of a newspaper, but I could not see what method could have been used that was so "devilish."

My uncle returned looking rather pleased with himself, in spite of the seriousness of his expression. He sat down and bellowed to the waiter to bring him another pot of coffee and then let his heavy head fall on his chest. His fingers seemed slightly clumsy as he pared tobacco from the thick brown twist he carried loose in his pocket. Looking across at him I thought, as often before, that he was built on a scale slightly larger than life. All his gestures were exaggerated. The job of filling his pipe seemed to require the use of all the muscular power of his arms, and when he lifted his coffee-cup I had a momentary vision of thousands of tankards in hundreds of public houses.

"Umph," he grunted, planting his legs firmly on the ground, "I don't know if I'm right but Joe thinks that there's every chance that I am. I'll know in about half an hour. However, we can't forget that we're here to attend a scientific congress and not to chase murderers. I've got to do some work on my exhibit and I also want to see Marshall's pea exhibit. He's a crank, but an amusing one, and can be guaranteed to have somethin' startlin', or at least startlin' to us scientists. This time he's got a theory that Mendel cheated on his results and that for all these years we've been paying lip-service to a cheat as the founder of our science. What he doesn't realise is that, whether Mendel did fiddle with his results or not, there is no doubt that he was one of the first people to give a direction to the study of heredity. I want to have a talk with him as I feel that a good argument with a stout opponent will clear my fuddled brain and enable me to concentrate on this damned problem. I may tell you that I wouldn't bother to find Porter's murderer if he had not done his murder in such a way as to spread suspicion among several people, and general suspicion clings to the innocent no less than to the guilty if we can't prove the guilt of one person."

He drove me up to the University and, to my surprise, his driving was unusually careful and he permitted several cars to pass him without entering into a furious race. I wondered whether he was ill but could not detect any signs of physical or mental weakness in his broad blunt face.

In the hall I was greeted by the janitor with a look of disapproval. "Mr. Blake, there is a gentleman to see you. He says he comes from the *Daily Courier*." A young man in a loud-checked tweed jacket and grey flannel trousers came forward. "Mr. Blake? Pleased to meet you. I came up here straight after I'd got your message but I couldn't find you and had to do the best I could by myself. Can you give me a few minutes now?"

I indicated that, difficult though it might be, I would do my best to give him a few minutes and led him over to the common-room and ordered more coffee, feeling that the Coffee Marketing Board, if there was such a thing, should present me with a medal as a prize consumer of the brew.

Macowen, as the young man introduced himself, only got as much out of me as I felt I could safely give without getting into trouble with Inspector Hargrave. I did not want to find myself in trouble for giving away evidence or for casting suspicion upon anyone before the police had prepared their evidence. However, I told him that I was going to write up my notes on the demonstration and he seemed to think that they would make a popular article and one that would be of educational value as well, for the *Courier* liked even its murders cultural. The murder of a scientist among scientists would receive far more notice than the murder of a grocer by common burglars.

When I left Macowen he was scribbling away violently in a reporter's notebook and was so engrossed in his story that he did not notice that his cigarette was nearly against his chin until it burned him, and he started and looked round him suspiciously before he realised what had happened. I went into the writing-room and worked up my notes of the previous day into a passable article.

With my article in my hand I went in search of Dr. Swartz. I found him in his demonstration room. The police had just permitted him to continue with his work and, as a result of the publicity he had received, there were queues waiting to have their blood grouped and their taste tested. Even the most staid and serious-minded scientists, who would as soon have thought of writing a popular book as they would have thought of ordering a scarlet flannel suit, did not seem to be able to resist the temptation of coming "to see where it happened." From the snatches of conversation I overheard I noticed a curious fact; this was, that none of them referred to the death of Porter as either "death" or "murder," but as "it," the definite words apparently seeming too definite and, somehow, faintly indecent.

Swartz, seated in a corner, had a bundle of the tasting forms in his hands and was shuffling them idly as he looked through them. He appeared to be trying to ignore the crowd that was pressing on all sides of him by pretending to be extremely busy. He acknowledged my greeting absently and took my article. He ran his eyes along the lines so quickly that I very much doubted whether he was reading them properly, but at the end he looked up at me and smiled. "Yes, I think that'll do. It's a fair popular statement of our work in this room."

He looked faintly worried and there were little wrinkles at the corners of his eyes. I did not think that he had slept well the previous night. "Business seems to be brisk," I remarked in an unnaturally loud and cheerful voice, and he looked round the room and dismissed the visitors with a wave of his pipe. "Oh, yes. But I wouldn't have had half this gathering but for the unfortunate death of Dr. Porter. I suppose I should thank him for the fact that I've already gotten more material than I hoped for during the whole Congress. What is it they say? 'Nothing in his life became him like the leaving of it.' That's right?"

For a moment he looked normal as he grinned sardonically, with the chewed bone mouthpiece of his corn-cob gripped between strong white teeth, then he looked back at the papers spread out before him and gathered them together into a bundle. With the air of one who had at last made a decision he rose to his feet. "Now I must go on down town and send a cable." The thought of sending the cable seemed to depress him still further and he was silent as we walked down the corridor together.

Just inside the front door we met Professor Silver. He still looked a little shaken but his hands were under control, no longer jumping about from button to button of his jacket or fiddling with his tie as they had been the previous day. He seemed to be anxious to speak to someone and stood in front of us so that we could not pass him, as I at least had intended to pass him, with a casual sympathetic nod.

His raucous voice was petulant as he cursed the police for their continual interference with him and he finished with an indignant triumphant screech, "Why they should think I would have anything to do with the death of poor Ian, I don't know. He was a brilliant man and had suffered from the jealousy of others who called themselves scientists but who were not above stealing from him when they thought they could do it without detection."

Dr. Swartz coughed, a cough that gave me the impression that it was covering a laugh, and Silver looked at him suspiciously before continuing. "But they've found out that I couldn't have done it. They asked the janitor at the door when he'd last seen Ian and he told them that he'd last seen him telling me to be quick, as he wanted my help. Hugh." He cleared his throat faintly. "And so they know it couldn't have been me. That doctor they've got wouldn't swear how long Ian had been dead, the fool, but they can't say I killed my friend, can they?" His eager face was thrust into mine and I felt very uncomfortable. He caught hold of my jacket.

Dr. Swartz took my arm. "Come on, Blake, I must hurry if I'm to send off my cable and do any work this morning. Sorry, Silver, we can't stop at the moment." He pulled me along beside him and as we went out of the door I was aware of Silver glowering at our backs. I walked to the entrance with Dr. Swartz and then, feeling that I had given Silver enough time to leave the door, I started back towards the chemistry department.

Round a corner of the building I heard the booming of a familiar voice, like waves thundering on a sandy beach, and realised that Uncle John was in the vicinity. He came stumping round the corner, with Dr. Flanagan on one side of him and Inspector Hargrave on the other. "You can see the trouble," he was bellowing. "This place is like a warren with its numerous entries. They have a janitor at the main door, but he's mostly there for show and to take messages. Anyone could get in or out without bein' seen if they wanted to. So no one can be said to have an alibi who cannot prove their presence somewhere

else during the whole time that the demonstration room was empty, or
at least was supposed to be empty except for Porter. Joe Flanagan
won't say how long he had been dead when examined—'Some time'
—Humph, and when we ask him how long he means by his 'some
time' he says, 'anythin' between twenty minutes and an hour,' and that
the room was too hot for him to give anything nearer. Hum-hum." He
buzzed like a furious bee stuck in a flower, and Dr. Flanagan looked
up at him indignantly. "It's all very well for you to speak, John Stubbs,
but if I risked a more exact estimate it might result in a serious
injustice which would do more harm than good, unless you'd just like
to see someone hang and never mind who it was."

Inspector Hargrave nodded his head wisely, like a young straggly
owl trying to behave like the solemn king of the oak. My uncle caught
sight of me and, with a gesture that seemed to sweep the buildings
from the ground, roared "Look at him. He's got no proper alibi and he
had a row with Porter the night before. The young fool then gets cold
feet when he realises that someone has been brewing their cyanide in
the place he chose for his quiet meditation and he behaves like a silly
version of Brer Rabbit—'lyin' low and sayin' nuffin'.'"

The inspector looked over towards me and beckoned with his hand.
Unwillingly I approached him. He smiled at me in a wintry fashion.
"Er, good morning, Mr. Blake. I just wanted to tell you that it was not
very wise of you not to mention to the sergeant that you had found
where someone had been preparing cyanide. If your uncle had not
informed me of your discovery and I had found it for myself I could
not have been blamed for drawing the obvious conclusion that you
knew more about the rest of the affair than you had told me. Your
uncle vouches for the fact that you are not a chemist and Jenkins
watched you looking it up in the *Encyclopaedia Britannica*, so that,
for the present, I don't think there is any need for us to worry further
about your misdemeanours, but if you conceal anything else that
comes to your knowledge I will be forced to look upon it more
seriously."

While he was speaking I stood in front of him, moving from one foot
to the other, like a schoolboy being reprimanded by a schoolmaster.
My uncle started to laugh and I glared at him. "Your bottom's all right
this time," he bellowed, "but the next time I catch you tellin' lies
you'd better be careful. I can recommend a silk handkerchief between
your trousers and your pants. It breaks the force of the blow and
doesn't sound wrong." The inspector smiled weakly at his childish
joke, while Dr. Flanagan joined in the laughter at my expense. I
smiled at my uncle and he straightened his glasses and puffed out his

moustache. He looked more or less serious again, but his eyes, when I
caught them over the steel rims, twinkled.

"Well, we know how the murder was done now, but we're still no
nearer findin' out who done it or which reason out of many impelled
him to do it. Someone had taken a hypodermic and pierced Porter's
ear-drum with it; the syringe was filled with cyanide but Joe Flanagan
here says that there was no need for the cyanide as the shock of havin'
his drum pierced would have been sufficient to kill Porter without the
poison. *Embarrass des riches*. There's too much dam' cyanide about
this case and I don't like it, I don't like it at all."

His big face was puzzled. "Where was Swartz bound for?" he asked,
and in answer to my look of surprise, "Oh, it's all right, I'm not playin'
the detective with you. I looked in at the window on the far side of
that wing and saw right through to this side where your two heads
were bobbing towards the gate."

"He was going down-town to send off a cable, he said. He doesn't
seem to have slept well last night and I expect he thought the walk
would wake him up."

"Hmm, yes, that'll probably explain why he did not send it off from
the office. I wonder what it's about." He laughed. "I'm beginning to
get so curious about everyone that soon I'll start walkin' up to
strangers and askin' them to show me the contents of their pockets. I
expect you heard what I was sayin' as you came round the corner, eh?
Well, I've-been amusin' myself by drawin' up a rough time-table. The
times, mind you, are only approximate. Here it is."

From the bundle of papers in his poacher's pocket he withdrew a
large postcard which was covered with his minute legible writing. I
took it and glanced down it. It ran as follows:

12.45: Andrew Blake leaves demonstration room to search for a
quiet place in which to write up his notes.

1.5: Dr. Swartz departs in search of Powys, with whom he has
arranged to have lunch.

1.7: Janitor, delayed by telephone call, is leaving for lunch and hears
Porter asking Silver to be quick as he has a lot he wishes to do.

1.9: Mary Lewis, having tidied up, leaves and meets Peter Hatton
in the corridor. (Statement supported by Dr. Hatton.)

1.10 or thereabouts: Powys leaves Swartz alone for a few minutes
while he prepares his dogs' food.

1.30: Silver, obviously in a hurry, is seen by many people leaving
hostel, brandishing sheaf of papers.

1.40: Blake and Stubbs encounter Mary Lewis entering dining hall, and immediately after meet Peter Hatton, hurrying in the same direction.

1.42: Blake and Stubbs meet Silver, who has discovered the body of Ian Porter and proceed with him to demonstration room.

Notes: Evidence of janitor is evidence that Porter was alive at 1.20. Sergeant Jenkins timed on a walk from entrance hall to hostel and back manages journey in about seven and a half minutes each way. Silver, even hurrying, is unlikely to have done the journey at the same speed as a police-sergeant in good training, and we must allow him a few minutes to collect his papers. Therefore evidence of janitor and time would appear to clear Silver, unless it can be proved that he used some other method of travel, i.e., taxi or bicycle. Statement of Swartz that he remained beside dog-pen is unsupported: he would have had sufficient time to reach his demonstration room, spend five minutes there, and return before Powys discovered his absence. Statement of Blake likewise unsupported. (Note, if Blake's statement is to be accepted, it follows that the cyanide must have been prepared some time before he entered the lab., as he makes no mention of its distinctive odour.) Statements of Mary Lewis and Peter Hatton are supported by one another.

I looked up as I finished reading and my uncle beamed at me in a pleased way. I felt that everything was going according to some plan which he had all worked out in his mind. "Do you see anythin' suggestive in it?" he demanded fiercely. I shook my head as I had rather liked Swartz and I did not want to point the finger of suspicion towards him unless it was absolutely necessary, though it looked to me as though he would be asked to try to prove that he had not left the dogs during Powys' absence.

"By the way," the inspector looked at me, "when you hit Porter do you remember where you hit him? In the solar plexus? Um. Then, doctor, that doesn't explain the bruise on his chin. Unless he bumped it against something else or got into another row. You said, Professor Stubbs, that he was pretty well lit up, eh? And he was staggering—well, he *might* have fallen again or, more likely, he got into another row after he left you and someone poked him on the jaw to keep him quiet."

Uncle John beamed at me and his spectacles slid a further quarter of an inch down his nose. He tried to look very mysterious as he said, "You've all missed the suggestive points in my little time-table and my remarks on it." We looked at him expectantly but he shook his shaggy head, dexterously caught the glasses as they fell off his nose, and roared, "No, no, work it out for yourselves. I may be wrong and I

don't want you jeerin' at me afterwards for an old fool. All that I have
is on that piece of paper and you can find it as soon as I can. I don't
know whether you'll draw the same deductions as I do, but you may. I
want a lot more information than I have before I'll start mentionin'
names."

Inspector Hargrave looked at him with the sympathy which one
gives to an unfortunate lunatic who gives no real reason for certifica-
tion, and Dr. Flanagan shook his head with the air of having known
John Stubbs for a long time but of having rarely seen him as eccentric
as he was now. The inspector turned towards me. "Have you seen
Miss Lewis or Dr. Hatton," he asked, "I want to have a word with
them." My uncle replied for me. "They're lunching with me, Inspector, and I promise you that I'll deliver them into your hands undamaged."
He grinned villainously. "That sounds bad, doesn't it? Will that be all
right?" Rather grudgingly the inspector intimated that he supposed
that it would be all right and Uncle John laughed and said, "Don't look
so disgruntled, man. I won't eat them for my lunch and I won't stuff
them with stories to tell you, however tempted I am."

Dr. Flanagan looked at his wrist-watch and he and the inspector
went off together. My uncle grinned at me wickedly and when they
were out of hearing he stooped down to me with a conspiratorial wink
and bellowed in my ear, so loud that I clapped my hand over that
organ and was quite surprised to find that I had not followed Porter's
example and died of shock. "Heh. They think they're dealin' with a
crazy old man and they'll only tolerate his presence because he knows
the actors in this drama and they don't. As for anythin' the old man
may discover, well, they'll be glad to hear of it and their expert eyes
will examine it and decide if it's worth any further consideration, but,
of course, they don't expect much from me. I am not supposed to be a
detective and Joe Flanagan'll tell you I'm a damn' bad doctor with the
worst bedside manner that was ever seen, so naturally they can't
believe that I'll discover anythin' they can't. So I'll be as mysterious as
I can, for I dropped the Inspector one or two hints and he examined
them as if I was tryin' to pass off some pinchbeck as real 24-carat stuff
and gave them back to me. Now I've got to go and see a man about a
mouse." He hooted like a steam-tug and stumped away from me in the
direction of the outside exhibits.

I met Macowen, the newspaper man, in the hall when I entered it,
and I informed him that I had sent off my article on the blood and
taste-testing. He tried to pump me for further information about
Porter and the other people who had been mixed up in the affair, but I
managed to persuade him that I knew no more than I had already told

him and, also, knowing nothing, I could not tell him what the inspector had uncovered during the morning. I left him with the strong impression that the police had a clue and expected to make an arrest very shortly, a phrase which appeared to comfort him greatly, fitting into its proper place with a cheerful click.

Opening the door of a lecture room quietly I slid into the darkness and sat down at the back. The lecture was very strange as I could not understand much of it. Completely unfamiliar words were linked together with ordinary ones and I would think I was getting along beautifully when suddenly I would find myself lost in a wilderness of technicalities. However, the lecture was illustrating his lecture with slides and some of them were very pretty, looking like the early explosive paintings of Kandinsky, while others had the formal excellence of a low relief by Ben Nicholson or a plan of the Suez Canal. I amused myself by trying to invent stories about the slides as they slipped in and out, until clapping announced the end of the lecture and the lights went up. I went in search of my uncle and found him talking to an excited Frenchman. He did not introduce me, but took advantage of my appearance as an excuse for an affectionate farewell.

CHAPTER 7

NATURAL MAGIC

"Harrumff," my uncle blew out his moustache and looked round the table, like a jolly Christmas card uncle looking at all the nephews and nieces who have just had a good blow-out on ginger-pop and strawberry ices at his expense. His eyes fastened on Peter and Mary and he smiled benevolently.

"Humph you two," he bellowed, "I don't want to tread on your sand-castles or to throw stones in your glass-houses, but don't you think it would be a good idea if you were to tell me what really happened between one and two o'clock yesterday afternoon?" Peter glared at him indignantly, but he blew out his moustache and continued, "It's no use, Peter boy, you'll never make a good liar. I knew you were lyin' when you started off last night and then, I'm sorry for it, I led you on and asked you simple questions and you tied yourselves up. Remember I asked you what you thought of Cortet's cage? Yes? Well I knew you'd seen it earlier in the day and I knew, too, that Cortet was goin' to take it down town durin' lunch to have an alteration made. He'd spent the journey in thinkin' up what I believe Dr. Swartz would call a 'dingus,' some sort of gadget, and he was very excited at the thought of tryin' it out. Well, you see, my children, I met him again to-day and asked him how the alteration had gone. In the course of a long and exhaustin' conversation, I discovered that he had this cuteness, which will apparently make his cage the ace of cages, fitted at a blacksmith's in the town at about a quarter past one yesterday while he stood by in terror lest the smith should damage his darlin' child. Now, then, don't you agree with me that it would be better if you were good children and told me the truth. I'm not threatenin' you, but I more than suspect that Inspector Hargrave thinks there's something fishy about your story. I persuaded him to let you lunch with me first, before he started his Star Chamber proceedin's. It would be much better if you could go along with me after lunch and tell the inspector that you had lost your heads yesterday and now wished to tell him the truth."

He stopped and, taking them off, wiped his spectacles on the sleeve of his tweed jacket. Peter and Mary were looking at one another in dismay and their faces were so surprised that I almost wanted to laugh. Uncle John settled his glasses firmly on his nose and ordered cigars and cigarettes and beer, this last a trifle tentatively, as we had already drunk enough beer to fill a good-sized bath.

When they seemed at last to have made up their minds they both started at once and then stopped. They did this again and Uncle John, his voice surprisingly subdued, said, "Will you begin, please, Mary? Peter, don't interrupt unless you want to correct anythin'. Come on, now, Mary."

She smiled at him and lit a cigarette while we pared the ends off our cigars. "Dr. Swartz left the room," she began, hesitantly, "just after his two assistants and left me alone tidying up my test-tubes and swabs. I did it as quickly as I could for I knew that Dr. Porter was coming in to do some work and I did not want to be there when he came. He's been a bit too——" she stopped and my uncle suggested the word "pressing." "Yes, that's it, pressing. However, I was not quick enough and I had just finished when he came in. He was most unpleasant and when I tried to leave the room he stood in front of the door so that I would have needed to push him aside in order to get out. He said a great many unpleasant things and I told him that I—er—did not like them. He got very angry then and came towards me. Ugh. I saw his great stomach wobbling backwards and forwards and I got frightened and went backwards. I retreated until I found myself in a corner and then I tried to hit him but he caught my arm. Just then Peter came in and I think I screamed."

She stopped and Peter took her arm. Uncle John sucked at his cigar and rumbled, "You go on, then, Peter."

"Well, I found that the work I had to do was not going to keep me as long as I expected and I went along to the demonstration room to see whether by any chance Mary had not left yet. When I opened the door I saw Porter and asked him what the hell he was doing and told him to let go of Mary's wrist at once. He turned round to face me, still keeping hold of her, and grinning like an ape. He put his other hand on a chair and I told him to let go of her at once or I would hit him. He laughed and told me to go ahead so I tried to get at him, but he swung the chair at me and I had to dodge that. The weight of his blow threw him off his balance and he let go of Mary and grabbed at my tie. I saw then that I would stand no chance against him armed with that chair and as he stumbled I hit him as hard as I could on the point of the chin with a short jab of my right and he dropped on the floor and rolled over flat on his back. I was never more surprised in my life, for I hadn't thought I'd hit him hard enough to knock him cold like that. I thought for a moment I'd killed him, but when I bent over him I saw he'd be all right in a few minutes. Then this damn fool woman," he squeezed Mary's arm, "tells me that I shouldn't have done it and I lose my temper and tell her that she can have dear Ian and walk out on her. I walk around the corridors for a good while, cursing and swearing to myself until I've worked all the temper out of my system. Then I say to myself, 'Peter, my lad, you've made one hell of an ass of yourself and the best thing you can do is to find Mary and tell her you're sorry for being such a damn' fool!' I pull myself together and march back to the demonstration room, full to the neck of mildness and good intentions. I threw open the door and marched in with a come-to-my-arms-my-beamish-girl look on my face.

"If I may coin a phrase, you could have knocked me down with a feather when I saw Porter lying in a different position and I went over to him. I've read too many books with Reggie Fortune and Dr. Thorndyke not to know the smell of prussic acid when it is wafted to my nostrils. I never for a moment thought of the possibility of his having committed suicide. He wasn't that kind of man. Without thinking where she could have got the cyanide, I sort of jumped to the conclusion that Mary had been trying the effects of chemical food on the fat guinea-pig. I'm sorry, Mary." He turned to her and she smiled at him. "Then I thought I'd better find her quickly and, I don't know why, I ran round all the buildings before I decided that the common-room was the place to try. That's when I met you and Andrew, sir."

My uncle grunted and took a long drink from his tankard, and then he looked at Mary and, still in his strangely quiet tone, asked her, "What about you, Mary, do you feel you can go on now?" She nodded and went on in a stronger voice than before. "I didn't know what I was saying when I told Peter that he shouldn't have hit Dr. Porter, and then I was annoyed with him for being angry with me, and shouted after him that he could go to hell so far as I was concerned. I picked up the chair and put it straight beside the desk. I looked at Dr. Porter and felt that I didn't want to be there when he recovered. I was simply furious with Peter for walking out on me and I'm afraid that I went into the ladies' lavatory and sat down and had a good cry. After that I felt better and did my best to make my face look decent again. I was rather ashamed with myself for rowing with Peter about someone as unimportant as Dr. Porter was and I, too, made up my mind that I would find him and apologise. I went back to the demonstration room because I thought that if he too was feeling penitent he'd have gone back there and I never thought that Dr. Porter would have still been there. I'd have expected him to have gone into a corner somewhere to lick his wounds. Then I saw him lying there and smelled the cyanide. How did I know it was cyanide? Oh, I've known the smell for years, ever since my elder brother started collecting butterflies and had a cyanide killing-bottle. At any rate, when I saw that Dr. Porter was dead, I'm afraid that I, just the same as Peter had thought of me, jumped to the conclusion that Peter had come back and poured poison down Dr. Porter's throat. I left the room quickly and went back to the ladies' lavatory to think. Then I decided that I'd better find Peter, and ask him about it, as it did not seem likely that he'd have poured poison down Dr. Porter's throat while he was unconscious, and so I set off for the dining room as I thought he'd be there." She laughed gently and looked at Peter. "My mother has always told me that men are terrible brutes. The first time she had a row with father he marched out of the house and she didn't learn till a long time afterwards that all the time she had been imagining him pacing the streets in misery or looking longingly at the electric rails of the Tube, he had been up in town standing himself a super meal. When we're married, Peter, and have rows you can have fair warning that *I'm* going to do the job of slamming out of the house."

Peter laughed and looked at my uncle. "That's all there is to it, sir, and I can assure you that neither Mary nor I did the job. Do you acquit us?" Uncle John ran his blunt fingers through his mop of grey hair and took a deep breath.

"You young fools," he thundered, with a fierceness that was belied by the twinkle in his eyes, "I never thought you had been indulgin' in murder as one of the finer or domestic sciences. But I knew you were hidin' somethin' and I thought it was rather like this. Why the hell once you realised that you had made such complete and utter fools of yourselves you couldn't try and straighten things out by makin' a clean breast of the affair I can't understand. Your story clears up a great many points that have been puzzlin' the police. Joe Flanagan'll be pleased that he's found a reason for the bruise on Porter's chin which worried him all last night. What time, then, did you leave the room, Mary? About two or three minutes later than you originally stated? And after you found the body? Say twenty-five to two? And you, Peter? You don't know, but think you must have just about coincided with Mary. Um. That means, roughly, that someone murdered Porter between one-twelve and one-thirty. A period of eighteen minutes. Um-um. I'll need to do some thinkin'."

He took his card out of his pocket and made one or two alterations. Then he shook his hair out of his eyes. "I'm sorry that I'll need to hand you two over to the care of Inspector Hargrave, and I can't promise you that you'll have a pleasant time with him. Not unnaturally, he'll be a bit annoyed to find that you've been leadin' him up the garden path. I'll put in a word for you and ask him to let you down as lightly as possible." He seemed a little worried by the thought of the ordeal which he had prepared by wangling their story out of Mary and Peter. He filled his pipe slowly and scribbled on the back of an envelope which he shuffled to the front of his thick load of letters and papers. He took his pipe out of his mouth and scratched his head with the stem, whistling absently through his teeth as he wrote, so that a faint breeze agitated the fringes of his moustache.

When he had returned his papers to his pockets he looked at us as if he could hardly remember who we were and said, "I hope you will excuse me if I don't run you back to the University, but I've just seen that there is somethin' which needs to be looked into urgently. Your story has cleared up one or two points, but it has not yet eliminated the mysterious Mr. X; in fact, you seem to have made things easier for any Mr. X to kill Porter. Um, I don't believe in Mr. X, goin' round with a pocketful of cyanide, waitin' for a chance to bump off, as they say, the unpleasant Dr. Porter. I think that if there is an X he is someone to whom we have been talking. This seems to me to have been a very clumsy murder. I can't yet understand why there's so much dam' cyanide lyin' about the place. It doesn't seem necessary. There's enough to murder nearly the whole Congress in that vessel on the table, yet the murdered doesn't drink the stuff but has it shoved into his ear with a hypodermic. Ah-ha," his face brightened, "I think I've got the reason. Good-bye, Mary and Peter. Take Andrew along with you as moral support, and give the inspector this note from me."

He scribbled on a card he took out of his pocket and handed it to Mary. As we left the room I heard him shouting to the waiter to bring him more beer. I looked back and saw that he had cleared one side of the table and was emptying his pockets upon it, apparently searching for some note which he had mislaid.

We found the inspector in the front hall, walking up and down the paved floor like a polar bear which thuds from one end of its cage to the other. He looked relieved when he saw us and came forward politely. "Good afternoon, Miss Lewis and Dr. Hatton—oh, and Mr. Blake. I want a few further words with you about yesterday's affair. Will you come with me?" I did not know if I was included in the invitation but I tailed along, thinking I might as well see what was happening. We went into the room where we had all been questioned the previous afternoon.

Mary handed across her note from my uncle and between them they managed to get out their story, with rather less hesitation than they had shown when telling it for the first time at lunch. Inspector Hargrave gave them hell. I have rarely seen a man so angry. His cheeks went a dirty white in colour and there were tight lines on the skin, as pearly white as sinews in a butcher's shop. When at last he had finished neither of them looked as though they would ever dare to tell a lie for the rest of their lives. I felt nearly as shaken as they did, for he kept casting nasty glances in my direction whenever he referred, as he did about once a minute, to the sin of impeding the police in the execution of their duty, and cried to high heaven to ask how he was expected to solve a case when nearly everyone connected with it, for some reason of their own, kept back essential facts. He rather overdid his severe reprimand stuff, with the result that by the time he had finished with us it had passed from the serious stage, through the funny one, into the boring. The policeman with the note-book and pencil had a hard time keeping up with the flow of indignation. At last, however, he informed us that we could go, but with the warning that he would want to see us again later to make our marks at the end of our statements.

I felt a bit exhausted by the flow of verbiage and realised, also, that I had not yet written my daily article for the paper. Peter suggested a lecture for me as being one that I could work up into a pleasant popular article, so I accepted his suggestion without making any enquiries as to its subject, beyond ascertaining that it would not be miles above my head, and went into the lecture room he indicated.

The lecturer was having a grand time and was obviously enjoying himself. He had spent a long time tracking down the haemophilia in the European Royal Families and had apparently managed to prove that it had originated with Queen Victoria.* It made an extremely good story and I took down a great many notes on the Spanish Royal family and the Romanovs, blessing Peter for having remembered this lecture for me. I noticed that one or two people looked as though they did not think it "quite nice" of the lecturer to wash such regal dirty linen in public, but they did not carry their disapproval to the extent of leaving the room, but remained seated, nodding their heads wisely whenever the lecturer brought out a particularly good point in favour of his detective ability.

I was sorry when the lecture came to an end for I had really enjoyed it and I had been able to follow most of it, though I must admit that I wouldn't have liked to have pricked my finger when I left the room in case I should suddenly discover that I, too, was a "bleeder" and no one could do anything to save me. I went across to the common-room and wrote up my notes, laying stress on the fact that there was a possibility that Rasputin owed his power over the Russian Royal Family to some hypnotic control by which he lessened the haemophilic tendency of the Tsarovitch. The lecturer had thrown out this idea as an aside and when I had approached him at the end of his talk and had mentioned it, he had said, "I haven't given full consideration to that point but it seems to me to be the most likely reason for his ascendancy."

Posting my article in the box in the hall of the common-room, I went into the lounge and gave my order for tea, and read the *Manchester Guardian*. Suddenly there was a mild earthquake in my neighbourhood and, looking over the top of my paper I saw that I had been joined by my uncle. His gray hair looked as if it had been skilfully tangled by a bevy of kittens, and his short pipe was sending out a positive smokescreen.

---

*For verification of this fact see *Blood Royal*, J. B. S. Haldane, *Modern Quarterly*, London, 2, 1937.

I ordered another cup and poured it out for him. He seemed to be rather pleased with himself and was almost purring, but I did not say anything, knowing that if I was to question him he would immediately become mysterious, so I assumed an attitude of indifference. His laughter rumbled quietly and he leaned forward and roared, "Don't look so damned don't care, Andrew. I know that you're just burstin' to hear what I've found out. Ha." A gust of laughter nearly split my newspaper. "Ah, ha, well just for lookin' so damned nonchalant I've a good mind not to tell you what I've found. Oh, well, I'll take pity on your curiosity. I'm beginning to get a rough idea of the murderer, and am trying to see why the murder took place at that time. I've got a good idea that Inspector Hargrave has fixed upon *his* idea of the murderer."

To this statement I replied that I could not see who it was as Silver was cleared, I did not think that Swartz had done the deed and Peter and Mary had come across with the truth. "Um," he replied. "They've come across with the truth, as you put it, but you realise that while before they supported one another's story, now they've told the truth neither of them has an alibi and each of them had the opportunity and, probably, the wish to murder Porter. The inspector will realise this and will go for them again, but I don't think that he's fixed on any of these people as the murderer. No, I'm afraid that his idea is that it was done either by one, John Stubbs, with the aid of the favourite blow-pipe and a little magic, or else one Andrew Blake who has no alibi for the necessary period and who was in the room where the cyanide, or some cyanide if you'd rather, had been prepared."

He chuckled wickedly, "I rather like the idea of myself in the dock. It would make the hell of a good trial in the *Famous Trials Series*, but I think that the inspector has not yet worked out a suitable method for me to use in this murder."

It had not occurred to me that I might be seriously suspected of the murder of Porter, in spite of the fact that I had no alibi. I thought that my recent acquaintanceship with him would make it clear that I was not in a position to prepare a premeditated murder. Forgetting that I had laid my cigarette case down beside my tea-cup, I ran my hands absently through my pockets in search of it. I felt something solid in the centre of the funnel of paper which stuck out of my jacket pocket and, fishing for it with my finger and thumb, I drew it out.

In my hand I held a flat red morocco box, obviously brand new, which I had never seen before. I pressed the little nickel stud at the side and opened it. There, in a little bed prepared for it, lay a gleaming hyperdermic syringe. Wondering how it came to be in my

possession I picked it out of the box. Its glass chamber was nearly full
of some colourless liquid. I held it to my nose and took it away again
quickly, for the smell of bitter almonds informed me that it was full of
cyanide. My uncle across the table was breathing heavily and his lids
were half-dropped over sleepy eyes. I opened my mouth to say
something foolish about it being a pretty toy.

At that moment an arm came over my shoulder and grabbed my
wrist and a cold voice snapped, "I'll have that, please." I laid the
syringe gently on the table and turned to face the chilly voice.
Inspector Hargrave, accompanied by two policemen in uniform, stood
behind me. One of the policemen picked up the syringe, inside a
handkerchief. The inspector stepped forward and laid an official hand
upon my arm.

"Andrew Harvey Blake," he announced tersely, "I hold a warrant for
your arrest upon the charge of murdering Ian Farquhar Porter. It is
my duty to inform you that anything you say will be taken down and
may be used in evidence at your trial."

CHAPTER 8

PAWN IN CHECK

I COULD NOT THINK of anything to say for a moment, but just
looked around me in a bewildered fashion. I saw that the people all
around me were standing up and looking at me with considerable
interest. I dare say I should have felt flattered by the stir I was
creating and the attention which was being paid to me, but I realised
that I could have made the same effect in a simpler way, say by
walking through the room in my shirt tails.

As I thought of this I started to laugh. I had just remembered a
story about a friend of mine who had gone to the Paris opera in a
drunken state and had retired to be sick. Feeling slightly better, he
had noticed the mess he had made and thinking heavily that as an
intelligent Englishman he should not let down his country, he had
taken off his pants and, tearing them up, had swabbed up the mess,

flushing away the dirty pieces. Back in his seat he felt full of conscious virtue until the lights went up at the end of the first act and he realised that he had forgotten to replace his trousers after removing his pants.

Inspector Hargrave looked at me as if he suspected that I was trying to play the lunatic in the hope of getting a guilty but insane verdict. He took a tighter grip on my shoulder and I managed to pull myself together. "You are a damned fool," I said, "but if you want to arrest me I don't mind. In fact I don't see that I can do anything about it, but repeat that you are one of the damnedest fools I've ever met."

A policeman was busy writing all this down in a note-book, working his tongue furiously from one corner of his mouth to the other as he wrote. My uncle smiled at me in a friendly way and boomed, "I'll try and get myself ordained, Andrew, and will wangle things so as to give you your last words of comfort on the scaffold." His laughter echoed round the corners of the room.

This remark did not appear to me to be in the best of taste and looking at the gaping faces round me, I saw that they shared my point of view and one or two disapproving glances were blunted on Uncle John's elephantine backside. He winked at me ponderously, a lowering of one eyelid that contorted his whole face like one of the gargoyles on Notre Dame, and I mumbled something about the condemned man drinking a strong cup of tea and going out with a firm step. The policeman took all this down as if he was transcribing a direct revelation from Heaven.

Inspector Hargrave coughed and I left the lounge, as securely guarded as if I had been the crown jewels. I thought it was extremely tactless of the inspector to have made no arrangements for transport. He apparently assumed that I was going to walk through the streets complete with my escort and he seemed mildly annoyed when I informed him that if I was to be taken through the streets they would have to drag me and I would make as much noise as I possibly could, but that I would be willing to come quietly if he would order a taxi. He wagged a long finger under my nose and snapped, "You'll do as you're told, my lad."

"I expect this is the first time you've ever made an arrest you weren't certain you could prove," I remarked, and his expression told me that I was right. "Well, then," I continued, getting quite heated, "do I need to remind you that I am not guilty until I have been declared so after trial by a judge and jury? You are a stuck up jack-in-office and fortunately my hanging does not depend on your opinion." I felt quite light-headed and embroidered my theme at

considerable length, finishing up by telling him that if he was not
careful I would bring a summons for wrongful arrest against the police,
buttressing it with one for assault if either he or his men laid a rough
hand upon me.

Perhaps it was my certainty that I would not remain in prison for
long that had the effect of shaking his confidence, but, at any rate, he
cooled down and informed me that he had his duty to do, and took a
taxi down town to the chief police station. The formalities there did
not last long and I was gratified to find that they apparently considered me clean and did not order me to have a disinfecting bath, as I
believe is customary on such occasions.

Alone in my cell, feeling rather like some monk requesting a
brother to bring him the materials of illumination as, for a penance, he
could not stir, I asked whether I would be allowed to have my
fountain-pen and some paper out of the contents of my pockets, which
had been taken away from me and listed on the appropriate form.
After some palaver I was allowed to have the articles which I wanted,
and also a cigarette.

The syringe which I had found in my pocket worried me. It had
obviously been placed there for the purpose of incriminating me and I
did not like it at all. I wondered when it had been placed in my jacket
and realised that it might have been there all day without my noticing
it, for I could not remember putting my hand into it at all, except to
shove more papers in on top of those already there. The funnel that
the papers made meant that it would have been a simple job for
anyone to slide the morocco case down to the bottom of my pocket
without my noticing that anything was wrong. I wrote down a list of
the people with whom I had come in contact during the day and
realised that that was not going to help me much, for at some time I
had spoken to every one who was any way mixed up with the
elimination of Ian Farquhar Porter. When I had finished my notes I
came to the conclusion that responsibility for the murder rested with
Peter Hatton, Dr. Swartz or my uncle and I felt pretty angry with
them all if they thought it was a good joke to have me shut up in jail so
as to divert suspicion from themselves.

I looked gloomily at the economical furnishings of my cell and
compared them, to their disadvantage, with the comfort of my room in
the White Lion and, quite methodically, I cursed everything I could
think of, watched all the time by a policeman who seemed to be ready
to pounce on me if I moved quickly or seemed to be about to cut my
throat with my fountain-pen nib.

PART TWO

CHAPTER 1

YOU PAYS YOUR PENNY

THE CORONER POLISHED his rimless glasses carefully on a brown silk handkerchief, chosen to match his suit, and glared at the public benches at the back, quelling the mumbling of the spectators. He looked expectantly towards the jury and the foreman rose to his feet, gripping the edge of the desk in front of him. He cleared his throat quietly and detached one hand from the desk to fiddle with the dimpled puff of his new tie. "We find that the deceased was murdered by Andrew Harvey Blake," he said precisely and sat down again abruptly, uncertain what he and the rest of the jury were intended to do next.

Professor Stubbs, who was filling his pipe under cover of the man in front of him, rammed the tobacco down too hard and had to pick it out again and tamp it down more gently. He shook his head quickly and the tangle of grey hair fell down over his forehead. He got up heavily and walked heavily out of the court, and, as if automatically, pushed open the door of a pub a few yards along the street.

The barman drew him a pint of bitter and he carried it delicately over to a table in the corner and, after sitting down, he wiped the polished surface dry with the sleeve of his thick grey tweed jacket. Pulling his bundle of papers out of his pockets he chose a few from each wad and spread them out in front of him and started to move them about, so that a casual observer would have thought that he was playing some elaborate game of patience.

This fantastic card game did nothing to reassure him. Sucking the yellow fringe of his moustache he roared to the barman to bring him another pint, and, splitting open an envelope with his thumb he spread it out before him and started to write. When the document was finished he signed it and dated it. For a moment he sat looking into the amber depths of the beer in his tankard and then he swung it to his mouth and bumped it down hard on the polished table so that the other drinkers turned to watch the bulky old man lumbering from the bar.

He walked along the street until he came to the blue sign of the police station. Pushing on the swing doors he entered and asked the sergeant in charge if he could see Inspector Hargrave on a matter of the utmost importance. After a wait of a few minutes he was escorted along a stone-paved corridor and into a small simply furnished office, nearly as austere and comfortless as one of the cells.

The inspector half rose to his feet and gestured towards a wooden chair upon which the Professor seated himself heavily; the bentwood creaking in protest. "Good evening, Professor Stubbs. Can I do anything to help you? Would you like an interview with your nephew?" The inspector was gentle with the gentleness of one who, having triumphed, could afford to be magnanimous. He seemed to be well pleased with himself and was conscious of the congratulations of his superiors who had expressed their gratification at the speed with which he had solved his first murder case.

"Inspector Hargrave," the deep voice boomed like the calling of a bittern in the small room, "you are a fool. In fact, you almost qualify for the title of damned fool. You sit there lookin' like an overfed cat—one that has just stolen a chicken, purrin' away to yourself and full of satisfaction. You have the wrong man in custody. In fact, you have arrested the only one of us who could not have committed the murder. Oh, yes, I know that the coroner's jury congratulated you upon your astuteness and the old boy himself, who has never *thought* in his life, *thought* you had done a clever piece of work in untanglin' this mystery. All you have done is to tangle it a damn' sight worse than before."

He paused and dug his papers out of his jacket pocket, and waved them angrily in the face of the bewildered inspector.

"I can make out a better case against anyone of the other actors in this amateur melodrama than you have managed to make out against Andrew Blake. Silver, or Swartz if you like. Dr. Swartz had every reason for killin' Porter and has no alibi for the necessary period of time, *and* he has the necessary knowledge an' ability which Blake does not possess. Either Mary Lewis or Dr. Hatton had the opportunity, the knowledge and the motive. Can't you see, Inspector, that the method used means that Porter had some knowledge of the person who killed him. Can't you see that he wouldn't have let my nephew get near him."

The inspector looked at him in a polite but sceptical manner, as if to suggest that either the Professor, with his well-known weakness for beer, had taken too much, or else he was more than a little mad. Professor Stubbs leaned forward, blowing out his moustache with an angry snort. "I can't understand the reason for the glassful of poison, unless it was meant to make us think that Porter had taken a sip of it. The murderer fell down badly there, for Joe Flanagan recognised it for a red herrin' as soon as he looked inside the stomach. No poison there—obviously Porter had not taken poison internally but had been injected with it. Joe couldn't find a puncture to account for the idea of its havin' been injected, but, having always fancied myself as a murderer I quickly came to the conclusion that the ear was a distinct possibility, and I was right. Can't you see what that means?"

He crashed his closed fist down on the desk and the impact sent the inspector's papers flying about the room like Brobdingnagian confetti. Inspector Hargrave scowled at him and bent down to gather up the scattered sheets, but the Professor paid no attention to the scowl and repeated his question, waving his sheaf of papers under the official nose. "I don't see that it means much," replied the inspector grudgingly.

Professor Stubbs hoisted himself off the chair, which had been like a shooting stick to an ordinary sized man, and placed his hands on the edge of the desk. "Sir," he said coldly, "you are either a fool or a stubborn mule and I don't know that it is worth my while tryin' to deal with you, but before I leave you to find out your own mistakes, will you answer me this? Under what circumstances would you not be suspicious or startled if someone grabbed you by the ear? Think, man, what the hell would you think if I grabbed you by your donkey's lug?

"Oh, you'd be surprised, would you? Pah, you'd be surprised. I've no doubt you'd be surprised if I planted my foot in your beam-end and you'd be surprised if I took you by the hair and swung you round this room. If the devil came to you in the night and offered you the dominion of the earth I've no doubt but that you'd be 'surprised.'

"Hell, man, if I grabbed you by the lobe of the ear you'd be more than surprised, you would kick up a shindy and would try and hit me. *But*, if you were goin' to have your blood grouped you'd think nothin' of it if the person who was assistin' you took hold of your ear. Would you?"

The Professor was marking time as he spoke by stamping heavily on the floor and his glasses were balanced extremely precariously on the tip of his blunt nose. The papers in his hand were whisking rapidly to

and fro beneath the inspector's nose and that official mumbled something to the effect that perhaps there was something in what Professor
Stubbs was saying.

"Perhaps there's somethin' in what I'm sayin', is there? Humph.
What I'm tellin' you is fact, as much as a fingerprint. The murder of
Porter was not one of those which is planned and carried into
execution on the spur of the moment. It was quite well thought out.
The idea obviously was to pretend that the murderer was goin' to take
a drop of blood from Porter's ear and, substitutin' the hypodermic
syringe for the spring-lancet, rammed it into the drum. You've got the
same evidence as I have. Take a look at it? What was Porter goin' to do
in the demonstration-room? He was experimentin' with a new non-
coagulant. How is a man goin' to find out if he has somethin' that will
not allow the blood to solidify if he has no blood for his experiment.
Now if you'll keep your damn' fool mouth shut I am goin' to lecture
you until you see sense.

"I don't think you can doubt that the murderer intended to come
into the room and offer to help Porter. The cyanide in the glass was a
blind so that we would not think that the murder was committed by
one of Porter's intimates but by anyone in the whole wide world, or at
least anyone present at the congress. There's your reason for the
murder takin' place in this congress. It's the opposite of a sealed room
mystery, anyone could have done it and the murderer was trustin' to
the fact of Porter's unpopularity to spread suspicion as widely as
possible. But he made his mistake in his method. For some reason he
neglected to pour the cyanide down Porter's throat. If he had done
that it would have been in the stomach and there would have been
nothin' to make Joe Flanagan suspicious. We'd have suspected everyone who disliked Porter.

"The murderer obviously did not want us to know that, takin' a tip
from Hamlet's uncle, he poured a leperous distilment whose effect
holds such an enmity with blood of man into Porter's ear. He might
have expected Porter to jump as the needle pierced the drum,
breaking the needle which would remain a mute witness at the
entrance to the brain. He wanted to run no risk of this happenin' and
so he prepared in advance for any such an eventuality. The accident of
Porter bein' knocked out must have seemed to him a fortunate one, for
it meant that there would be no struggle or risk of a broken needle,
but having prepared his plans he did not trust himself to swerve from
them or to invent new plans on the spur of the moment. So, sure of
the absolute perfection of his original scheme, he went ahead on it.

"Now you see that the murderer must 'a' been someone who knew

Porter well enough to offer his services with the certainty of their being accepted. Either Dr. Hatton or Miss Lewis could have done that, for they were not to know that things would come to a state where Hatton would knock out Porter. Take Dr. Hatton, for instance, he has the knowledge necessary for the makin' of cyanide, he has worked on blood, so he'd be quite an acceptable assistant to Porter.

"Remember that until about five past one, neither of them liked the other, but there was no open break between them and Porter was the sort of man who would gain a lot of pleasure from bein' assisted by a man who hated him. It would have fed his vanity in a strange way. I knew the man and I had noticed that odd characteristic and Hatton had noticed it, too, knowin' that not one of Porter's assistants felt either affection or loyalty towards him. If it seems odd to you that this should be so, just think over the things I have told you about him—it is not likely that an assistant, if it could be hidden, would tell him of any new discovery, as one of my assistants would tell me, for that discovery would not be used for the benefit of science, but for the aggrandisement of one man, Dr. Ian Farquhar Porter. He got a great deal of pleasure out of the fact that people disliked him and that he was climbin' to fame on the shoulders of others. His idea was that if he became well enough known the people who disliked him would be forced to pay him lip-service, at least. He was goin' to blackmail his way into becoming an F.R.S., by becoming so well known that people who did not know of his methods would use him as a stick to beat the Royal Society, a favourite game, sayin' that their treatment of him was an example of professional jealousy. Oh yes, he'd have got his F.R.S. and all the rest of it. You must understand all this about the man if you are to understand why anyone of the three, Swartz, Hatton or Miss Lewis, might have been called in to act as his assistant. They would have felt uncomfortable but their discomfort would have added to his confidence.

"The murderer knew this and was countin' on it. In addition to this, however, the murderer has to be someone who could use the spring lancet. Now Swartz, Mary Lewis and Peter Hatton all answer to that requirement. *I* could do it, but Porter would not know I could. To him I was a plant physiologist, a botanist, who might be all right with a packet of seeds but helpless with a lancet. The one person who could not have done it is Andrew Blake. Would you ask me to take a finger-print? No? I thought not. Well, then no more would Porter have allowed a journalist to draw blood from him. However much he might have desired to murder Ian Porter, Andrew Blake would never have worked out the plan I have just outlined to you. There would have been no point in his doin' so, for he would never have got near to his victim."

Bowing to the Inspector, Professor Stubbs roared, "Therefore, gentleman of the jury, I demand an acquittal, havin' shown incontrovertibly that this murder is the one murder which the accused, Andrew Blake, could not have committed. The defense rests, m'Lord." He laid down his sheaf of papers and perched himself on the chair again, beaming benevolently over his glasses.

Inspector Hargrave remained silent for a moment and then held out his pouch towards the professor who was occupied in digging carbon out of his pipe with a broken penknife. "Ah, Professor Stubbs," he said, "I must admit that you have put up a very fair defence, very fair, and if there was nothing else I might be inclined to agree with you. But the case against Blake is just as strong as that which you have advanced in his favour. There was admittedly bad blood between him and Porter, and he had previously descended to violence, and then he was in contact with the apparatus with which the cyanide was prepared and, this is a telling point, his were the only finger-prints on the polished sides of the syringe."

Putting a match to his pipe, Professor Stubbs sighed deeply and then spoke very slowly as if to a child, stressing each word with a thump on the desk from his closed fist, "I have just shown you that it would have been absolutely impossible for him to kill Porter in the way he was killed and you still insist upon pullin' up one or two odd links and pretendin' that you are in possession of a chain. Look at your evidence, man, and you'll see that a good counsel will knock it to pieces in five minutes. Of course the only finger-prints on the syringe were Blake's—it had been planted in his pocket, he found it and fiddled about with it and dozens of people saw him do that. The person who placed it in Blake's pocket wasn't goin' to have his finger-prints on it—if he did that he might just as well have 'This is the property of John Doe' engraved on it, substituting his name for that of Doe. Come on, admit that your case falls to bits."

The blotting pad in front of the inspector was covered with scrawls of all sorts and shapes. Poising his pencil delicately he carefully added a pair of squinting eyes to a pig and did not look up. "I won't say that you're not right, Professor, but I'll need to see my superior before I can do anything further regarding this new evidence which you have provided me with. Now can you tell me anything about the other people, anything, that is, which I don't already know? This American fellow now, Swartz—that's the German for black, isn't it? Well, do you think he could have done the murder?"

Beneath their eaves of heavy grey hair the Professor's eyes twinkled. "Inspector," he said solemnly, "I could show you that anyone you'd care to name had done the murder. I could probably prove that I'd done it myself and I'd prove it with such a wealth of detail that you would have no hesitation in arresting me. Then, of course, just as easily, I would prove that it was absolutely impossible for me to have done it and you would have to let me go again. In fact, I would like to have a shot at provin' that the unpleasant Dr. Porter was murdered by that intelligent young police officer, Inspector Hargrave."

Uncertain whether the word "intelligent" was intended as a cut for his credulousness, Inspector Hargrave flushed slightly and shuffled his feet. Then with a gesture of impatience he clicked his fingers, as if to indicate that he had had enough fooling and wanted to get down to business.

"Humph," the Professor snorted, "so you want to make Swartz guilty, do you? Well, that should be easy enough. He had a motive, a stronger motive no doubt than any of the others we've heard about, and he had the opportunity. Let's pretend we're watchin' Swartz murderin' Porter. To begin with, he's an American and it is unlikely that he would take a special voyage over here in order to murder Porter, so he seizes upon this congress as a suitable stage for his deed. When he arrives here he discovers that Porter has been workin' on a new non-coagulant and this suggests the scheme to him, and he says somethin' like, 'Look here, my demonstration-room is all fitted up for blood-groupin', so if you wish to give your stuff a trial while you're here, why not just drop in sometime, for it'll be easier than workin' just anywhere.' Porter, being Porter, thinks this offer is just a part of what is due to him as a great man and he grandly remarks that he'll drop in sometime. Swartz sits down and does a bit of hard thinkin' and eventually hits on the plan we've already looked at. Then there is the problem of gettin' hold of poison and it occurs to him that as he's been lucky enough to be planted in the middle of the Chemistry Department of the University, the best thing he can do is to prepare the poison out of that Department's materials in one of their rooms, and he looks around and is lucky again for he finds a well-stocked unoccupied lab., apparently just made for his purpose. There is a key in the door of the lab. so, while his distilling operations are in progress, he locks the door and if anyone tries to get in they assume that the door has been locked by the janitor. He works in rubber gloves so as to leave no finger-prints and when he's finished he leaves the apparatus set up, to show that someone has been makin' cyanide and to provide the police with a nice clue so that they won't come chasin' around after everyone to see who has had cyanide.

"Now he's all set and all he's got to do is to wait for a favourable opportunity. When Porter asks him if he can use the demonstration room durin' the lunch hour, he wonders if this can be the opportunity which he has wanted. He goes along to see Powys, with whom he has arranged to have lunch and chats with him for a few minutes. Then, just as he's going to excuse himself to go and wash his hands, or something of the sort, the convenient Powys says, 'Just a mo' before we go off. I must feed the dogs. Wait here for me, it'll only take a few minutes.' Swartz nods and says he'll amuse himself by looking at the dogs.

As soon as Powys has gone Swartz sprints round to his room and strolls in, ready to excuse himself if Silver is there with Porter. To his surprise Porter is lying on the floor, knocked out. Perhaps he is beginning to stir a little. To Swartz this seems a blessing as it means that he will not need to waste any time on palaver before he does the deed. He injects his cyanide into Porter, pours the rest of it into one of his little glasses, arranges the body artistically, and hastily fills up one of the taste-testing forms to show where Porter had reached when he drunk the cyanide. Then he dashes back to see Powys, slowing down to a stroll and again he has some excuse ready if Powys is there before him. However, he is back first and he climbs into the pen and starts playin' with the puppies. Powys returns and sees Swartz in the middle of the dogs and assumes that he has not left the pen.

"Then they go off to lunch together. Swartz probably thinks of throwin' away all the evidence that he still carries with him, but, on second thoughts, he decides that he'll keep the syringe, loaded with cyanide as a good red herring if the police get curious about him. It occurs to him that the one alibiless (is that a new word?) person against whom it would be impossible to get a conviction is my nephew, and he comes to the conclusion that a few days in gaol won't do Blake any harm, while, ten days or less from now, he will be on his way back to America and though, once Andrew Blake is cleared, suspicion may fall on him, there is no direct evidence to connect him with the murder and he doubts if the police will bother about extradition when they can't be at all certain of obtaining a conviction.

"So, laughin' to himself, he walks beside Blake through the corridors and drops the hypodermic syringe down the funnel made by the papers, at the same time bumpin' against him so that he will not notice the arrival of the foreign body in his pocket. By this time he knows that Andrew Blake, having read the subject up in the *Encyclo-paedia Britannica*, has recognised that the apparatus in the room he chanced to use was used for making cyanide and has been afraid to tell the police that he has recognised it, in case they suspect him, a fact that will tell against him in the mind of Inspector Hargrave.

"Havin' everythin' arranged so neatly Swartz just sits back and waits for the end of the congress, when he will return to America feelin' that he has done some extremely good work while in England. There is no reason for him to worry for there is no fear of Andrew Blake bein' hanged as some cunnin' barrister, or that old fox John Stubbs, is bound to hit on the fact that of everyone at the Congress, Blake is the least likely to have done the murder, and that it is impossible for him to have done it as his weapon is the pen and could never be the hypodermic syringe.

"There, then, is your case against Swartz, q.e.d. I can't say that I like it. There are far too many lucky accidents in it, but you wanted a case and I've given it to you and I may tell you that it is a far stronger case than the one you have put up against my nephew. It is at least made of good stout cardboard, while your case is built of rice-paper and will melt the first time it gets damp."

Taking a gaudy coloured handkerchief from his breast pocket, Inspector Hargrave mopped his forehead, and looked up, his face rather brighter than before. "If you don't mind my saying so, Professor Stubbs, I think you've got something there. Of course, there are a lot of gaps in your story, but I dare say we'll be able to fill them. It's surprising how much evidence you can unearth once you have a line to work upon. It's getting the line that is the real job, for as you will realise, we in the Force work at a disadvantage. The spectator who watches the whole of the game should be better at describing it than the man who is called in to commentate on the second half only. You know all the people who are mixed up in this affair and you know how they would behave in certain circumstances, where I can only judge them by what I've seen under admittedly difficult circumstances. You can have no idea, Professor, how grateful I am to you for your assistance and I will certainly ask my superiors to review the case of Andrew Blake in the light of this new evidence, first thing to-morrow morning."

Professor Stubbs' eyes twinkled as he looked over the tops of his glasses. "Inspector Hargrave," he said softly, "you are not forgettin' that I told you that I could make out an equally good case against myself, Professor Silver, Mary Lewis, or Dr. Hatton, are you? I wouldn't forget that."

The Inspector laughed cheerfully. "You must have your little joke, eh, Professor? Well, I must say that the case you've given me is good enough for the time being. I always had my doubts about that American."

Gathering up his sheaf of documents the Professor stuffed them into his pocket and, nodding at the Inspector with the gawkiness of a friendly Great Auk, stamped out of the office and along the stone-paved corridor. Inspector Hargrave listened until the footsteps had died away and then, after sharpening his pencil with an old razor-blade, he took some sheets of paper out of a drawer and started to write.

CHAPTER 2

YOU TAKES YOUR CHOICE

ANDREW BLAKE sat on the edge of his bunk and swung his legs and looked out at the patch of blue sky that informed him that it was a fine day. Being in prison, he decided, was not really so bad after all. They had been inclined to be a little tough with him at first, but for some reason or other they had become more gentle as time went on and in the middle of the evening Inspector Hargrave had actually come along and inquired how he was getting on. After that he had been given his cigarettes and matches and the top of a tin of Barneys as an ash-tray, and they had allowed him to read a book.

He was mildly annoyed with his uncle for neglecting to pay him a visit to liven him up in his cell. It was only when he remembered that he was in prison on a charge of murdering Dr. Porter that he felt rather uncomfortable, for he was forced to admit that if you looked at it one way, the evidence against him was fairly strong and now the coroner, a nasty prim little man, had done his best to back the police up in their wrongness. Several times during the night he had woken up suddenly with the feeling that he was falling through space, and he had stayed awake for a long time, wondering whether he could have murdered Porter and then forgotten all about it. It did not seem possible, for one did not go around committing murders in an absent-minded way, however many cigarettes one could light without noticing it.

He had always believed that prisoners were fed on skilly and grey bread, and so was pleasantly surprised when the police officer brought him bacon and eggs, toast, butter and marmalade and coffee on a tray from a nearby restaurant. He gathered that before his trial a prisoner was treated as if he was a normal man who had to be locked up but who was otherwise all right. The policeman who was acting as warder was, if possible, even more polite than he had been the previous night.

When he had eaten his breakfast and was wondering how he was to get a shave, for his face felt rather like a newly-mowed cornfield, the warder came to the door and, unlocking it with a clank of vast keys, pushed his head in, announcing, "A visitor to see you, Mr. Blake."

Professor Stubbs, looking even more untidy than he had done the previous afternoon, stumped into the cell and dumped himself on the edge of the bunk, which groaned under his weight, having been made for men of more normal proportions. "Humph," he snorted, "sleep well? How do you like being shut up? Have you tried stretchin' your neck to accustom it to the rope? A man called John Lee once managed to get away as they failed to hang him three times. This was taken as proof of his innocence, but Charles Duff, in his *Handbook on Hanging,* suggests that it was a heredity immunity. Ha."

He laughed and it sounded as if a whole brass band had been shut up in the little cell. Andrew looked at his uncle sternly. "I do not think that all this talk about hanging is in the best of taste. I have no wish to try conclusions with a gallows and I hope that the occasion for me to do so is still very far distant."

"Oh, I don't think that this affair is goin' to go any further. Humph, I came along here last night and had an interview with Inspector Hargrave and, I think, I convinced him that whoever did the murder, it could not have been you, as you have not the technical skill necessary to have done this murder. I offered to prove that anyone of us others could have done it and he was so excited that he almost had tears in his eyes as he thanked me for my help. Oh, they'll let you out soon as they'll see that the case against you has fallen to nothin'. I may have led the Inspector up the garden path, but it's all in a good cause. I *think* I now know who murdered Porter, so that, if I'm right, it's who and when and how answered. I've still got to find the answer to why and then I think I may get the proof I need. Ha, I see from your expression that you don't believe me? Of course, I'm just an amateur at this game and can't be expected to enter into competition with the police on their own ground. I've been readin' about murders, the most impossible murders, the more impossible the better, for donkey's years, and now I have a good plain murder dumped down under my nose with plenty of nice suspects, and I want to be clever about it. I would like a murder of a man in a sealed room, so the only murder I get is the opposite of that. A man alone in a room to which about twelve hundred people have had free access."

While he spoke the professor slapped his knees noisily and the warder, who had remained at the door, looked at him suspiciously as if he thought that this noise was cover for some other noise, such as the passing of a file. "Murder," announced Professor Stubbs boisterously, "is great fun when you don't like the murdered, and I can't pretend that I liked Porter, but it looks to me as though the murderer might be someone whom we don't dislike." He got up. "I must now go and take a look at my plants, for, after all, I came here to show them off, not to track down crime. 'Crime doesn't pay' we're told. Well, I certainly seem to have wasted a lot of time on it, but I consider that I'm well paid if I can work out the puzzle to my satisfaction."

His step military in its precision, Inspector Hargrave snapped into the cell immediately Professor Stubbs had left it. "Good morning, Mr. Blake. I've got good news for you. Owing to the fact that fresh evidence has come to light I have informed my superiors that I wished to discharge you. You will understand that you are not to leave town without informing us."

"Why? Have you found the murderer?"

The inspector slapped his hands together briskly, the gesture of an Eastern potentate requiring the presence of one of his slaves. "Well, of course you will understand that I cannot give away anything at the present time, but I can tell you this. We have a strong suspicion, almost amounting to a certainty, that a certain gentleman is neither so innocent nor so guileless as he would have us believe. It is merely a matter of hours before we are in a position to make an arrest. Once we have tied up a few loose ends everything will slip into place and we will have as neat a case as you can desire. A case that even your uncle, with all his cleverness, won't be able to demolish. We are very grateful to Professor Stubbs, but you must admit that he is inclined to be too clever by half." He paused and rolled the phrase over on his tongue appreciatively, repeating it, "Too clever by half. If you will come with me now, Mr. Blake, we will go through the formalities of giving you back your things and discharging you."

When Andrew had finished with the official formalities and could once again jangle his loose change in his pockets, he went out to the front of the police station. He heard a familiar voice declaiming and saw his uncle leaning on the desk in front of the sergeant. "Beer," he was shouting, "varies more than any other drink and is more of a gamble. You know that a bottle of a certain wine of a certain vintage should be drinkable, but you go into a strange pub and order a pint of four-ale you got no surety that it'll be any good. The pub-keeper may not take care of his pipes, his cellar may not be the right temperature. The beer may be sour or flat or one of a million other things. Beer, I tell you, is the hell of an undependable drink."

He crashed his fist down on the desk, so that ink pots, pens and blotting-pads jumped, and turned round to face Andrew. "Humph, so they've let you out, have they? You've been robbed of your place in the *Famous Trials* series. That's hard luck. I've just been telling this dolt," he looked at the sergeant and grinned, his eyes twinkling over the top of his glasses, "telling this dolt a few facts about beer. In spite of the fact that he drinks it, an Englishman knows nothing about his national drink. He is afraid to admit that beer can vary in case someone accuses him of being fussy. My God," he exploded and spread out his arms in a sweeping gesture which prompted the sergeant to put his hand on the ink-bottle, "My God, why should people be ashamed of knowin' what they're drinkin'? Go to France and you will find that the simplest labourer knows more about the wine he drinks with his lunch. So far as the Englishman is concerned, his beer might be a chemical compound that started its life in a laboratory at the other end of a pump, and it often tastes as if it was. Pah, and they have the damned effrontery to be proud, yes, proud, of their ignorance. When I murder someone my motive will be that the murdered was proud of his ignorance." He glared fiercely at the sergeant, blowing out his moustache. "The next time you take a glass of beer, my good fellow, think of it as a drink and not as a medicine. Instead of ramming it back into your stomach—a disgustin' German students' trick—try tastin' it. Yes, I said try *tastin'* it. Don't look so damned surprised. It won't poison you and you'll learn to enjoy it for its own sake."

With a jerk of his hand the professor gestured to Andrew to follow him and swept out of the police station, if someone shaped rather like a heavy tank can be described as sweeping out of anywhere.

Inspector Hargrave, his lips twisted with a suppressed smile, listened to the machine-gun chatter of the Bentley as it heated up and then the slash of gears and the roar as it started off. When the noise of departure had become no louder than the distant rumble of artillery, he shook his head slowly, as if mourning over the fact that a clever man like Professor Stubbs should be mad.

Pursing his mouth into the shape of a violet the inspector whistled slowly and walked back to his room. He sat down at his desk and looked at the sheets of paper, over which he had sat for half the night. He scribbled for some time and then read through the results of his work, lighting a cigarette to help him to think. When he laid down the sheets of paper he lay back in his chair for a few minutes with his eyes closed, one finger stroking the wispy straw-coloured moustache on his lip. Suddenly he came to a decision and leaned forward, stubbing out the glowing end in his ashtray, and picked up the telephone. "Please tell Sergeant Jenkins that I want to see him, and ask him to bring along his notes on the Porter case."

The sergeant entered the room. "Good morning, Inspector, I see you've let Blake go. The case against him collapsed?" The inspector was short with his subordinate, passing on the abrupt manner of his superiors when they had reprimanded him for making an arrest without a sufficiency of evidence. However, as he finished he thawed a little and provided Jenkins with an outline of the case he had built up from Professor Stubbs' remarks on Swartz, "So I think the best thing we can do is to go up to the University and see what this American has to say for himself. I don't mind telling you that I think we've got a pretty strong case against him. We'll ask him a few questions and just see if his answers tally with his earliest statements. If they don't ... well. . . ."

At the University everything seemed to be going on as though nothing had happened, no longer were there little knots of men chattering in the hall and the name Porter was as nearly forgotten as that of Erasmus Paviom or John Dereham. Even the janitor did not straighten up into a military alertness, but merely nodded in an offhand way to the inspector and sergeant as they walked into his cubby. "Is Dr. Swartz in this morning?" snapped the inspector, faintly nettled by the man's negligence. The janitor did not even bother to enunciate clearly as he mumbled, "Can't say. I haven't seen him, but then this damn' place has as many entrances as a damn' honeycomb." The word he used was not "damn" and the inspector looked a trifle shocked and said sharply, "Don't swear when you talk to me." The janitor scowled but did not reply.

Inspector Hargrave, followed closely by the sergeant, walked smartly along the corridors, and as they went their shoes clicked on the stone flags like the shoes of a pony on a frosty road. The door of the demonstration room was open and they walked in. Mary Lewis was working at her bench and the two assistants were there, a few people were being tested for their blood-groups and tasting ability, but there were no signs of Dr. Swartz. The inspector walked over to Mary and waited until she had finished stirring up some drops of blood on slides. "Excuse me, Miss Lewis," he said, and she laid down the glass rod on a piece of filter-paper and turned round. "Have you seen Dr. Swartz this morning? I wanted to ask him a few questions."

"No, I'm sorry none of us have seen him this morning. I wonder what can have happened to him. Of course, he may have taken the morning off from this to go round the other demonstrations and exhibits, or he may have gone to hear a paper read, but I'd have thought that he would have looked in here just to tell us where he would be in case we needed him. However, I expect he'll be in soon and, if you like, I'll tell him that you were looking for him. How will that do?"

"I'm afraid, Miss, that we want to see him rather urgently. You are sure you have no ideas where he can be? No?" He turned towards the two assistants, "What about you? Neither of you have any idea where Dr. Swartz is? Hmm."

He turned sharply and left the room, Sergeant Jenkins trailing along behind him, like a wooden dog on wheels. They walked to the janitor's cubby-hole. Inspector Hargrave, ignoring the clucks of protest from the outraged custodian, picked up the telephone directory and thumbed his way through it until he found the number he required. He dialed and listened to the buzz at the other end. "Hello, is that Dalston Hostel? Can you get Dr. Herman Swartz for me? What? Say that again. His room has not been slept in? No. That'll do."

He slammed down the receiver and glared at the empurpled janitor. "Come on, Jenkins, we must get back to town. Our man's done a bunk and we'll need to get a warrant or he'll skip. It's a blasted nuisance, for we haven't got a complete case against him and we'll need to do all the work after he's inside."

A loud voice boomed through the hall into the booth. "All hail, Inspector Hornley," it cried jocularly, "how goes the investigation? Are you ready to hang the whole Congress for a conspiracy to murder Ian Porter? What, has someone stolen your toffee-apple? Don't look so glum or I'll need to ask Joe Flanagan to give you a dose. Is your inside in tune with the universe? Does inner cleanliness come first? Which sleep-group do you belong to and do you suffer from night-starvation?"

Professor Stubbs, with a copy of the *Daily Courier* crumpled under his arm, was looking very cheerful as he quoted from the advertisement columns. Mentally, the inspector compared him with a well-fed

Persian cat which would purr at the earliest opportunity. The stream of tender enquiries after his bile ducts and sluggish liver continued. He swore, using the same words for which, earlier, he had rebuked the janitor. "Have you seen the man Swartz, Professor?" he barked, in a parade-ground manner that any military commissioner of police would have admired.

"No. Why?" Professor Stubbs' face was as innocent as that of an overfed grizzly bear. "Why? Damn and blast him, he's disappeared. In connection with what you were telling me last night I wanted to ask him a few questions. Looks as if your suspicions were right after all, doesn't it, eh?"

"Looks like it? Well, yes," the professor's voice was low and his usually fat and creaseless forehead was wrinkled by a frown. He shook himself and growled fiercely. "Why the hell did I want to be clever? Oh, I was so cunnin' and now this has happened. I must be right and yet. . . ." He seemed to be speaking to himself and the inspector looked at him suspiciously, and seemed to be just on the point of questioning him as to whether he had made any indiscreet remarks to Dr. Swartz, when he burst out violently, tossing the grey hair back from his eyes, "You must find him, Inspector, and find him quickly. That is imperative. Put every man you can spare on to the job, and for God's sake don't waste a minute."

The inspector was slightly stiff and his tone rebuked, "I know my duty, Professor Stubbs, and you can rest assured that we will waste no time in locating Dr. Swartz. I am just about to proceed down town to apply for a warrant."

Looking at him gloomily out of one bird-like eye, the professor grunted, "Apply for your warrant if you want to, but I doubt if it'll be much use." Inspector Hargrave was puzzled by this statement but had no time to ask further questions, for the professor, ignoring his motions of protest, shooed him and Sergeant Jenkins out of the hall and into the street, and, stopping a passing taxi, bundled them into it, panting, "You can charge this to me if it's questioned on your expenses sheet. For God's sake find Swartz as quickly as possible. If you hurry you may be in time to prevent another murder."

As the taxi drew away from the kerb Inspector Hargrave glanced at the professor's face. It was greyish-white in colour and distinct separate drops of sweat were distributed about the cheek-bones, like specks of dew on a spider's web. He turned to the sergeant. "Hm, so there'll be another murder if we don't hurry, will there indeed? If I'm not mistaken, Jenkins, I'd say that the learned and scatterbrained Professor knows too damn much about this affair and is afraid that he'll be the next victim. I wouldn't have thought that he was the sort of man to be so easily scared, but then it only goes to show that you can't judge a man from his appearances. The big bluff professor with all his shouting is only a windbag after all, and one that's punctured by the first threatening of personal danger—not that I believe for a moment that he's in danger. Well, he's frightened all right, and it's up to us to find Swartz and put his mind at rest, bless him."

"Ah," said Jenkins, profoundly, "it only goes to show, as you say, sir. You know, sir, I never did like that American. He was holding something back all the time he was speaking. I think, sir," he added, diplomatically, remembering that it was not good to have sergeants more astute than their inspectors, "that you mentioned something about it at the time, didn't you?"

"Yes, I believe I did," replied the inspector, drawing on a non-existent store of memory. "It's strange how often one's first impressions prove right, after all. I don't think we can have any doubt now as to the identity of the murderer. He's more or less declared his guilt by doing a bunk. I don't think we'll have any difficulty in getting our warrant. Ah, here we are. While I see about the warrant, will you look up the sailings of ships to America? Don't forget the cargo-boats. He'll expect us to try the liners and will probably try to get a passage on a freighter. If we manage to catch him before he sails it'll save the expense of extradition, as well as the time that would take. I'll expect you to have all the necessary information by the time I've got my warrant."

For a man who was supposed to be in terror lest a bogyman should jump out of a corner and stick a knife in his ribs, the behaviour of Professor Stubbs was rash in the extreme. His short pipe sending up showers of sparks, he stumped along the corridors, excusing himself briefly when he blundered into lectures. In any unoccupied room he wandered round, peering short-sightedly into cupboards and under benches. He picked up a length of glass-tubing in an unoccupied laboratory and used it as a probe in his searching under benches, and when its point hit anything he bent down and pulled out the obstruction, usually an empty box or a bundle of scientific publications.

When he had finished with the chemistry department he worked his way through those devoted to zoology and biology, ticking each room off on a plan he scribbled on the reverse side of the abstract of a paper on rust in wheat, and methodically noting the rooms which were occupied, so as to pay them a visit later, during lunch time, when no one would be there. Eventually he came to the smallest of the departments, that which the University had set aside for those

students who wished to study genetics and to know more about the
heredity of themselves and their fellow-creatures than was considered
to be quite nice. For, although the University was proud to have a
Congress of Geneticists meeting in its buildings, as a prestige-bringer,
yet it did not consider that the science of genetics had had time to
prove itself. Dating only from the early 1900s as an organised study, it
had not yet acquired the requisite number of generations of grey-
beards that would put it on a level with the other sciences.

The Senate of the University, classical by tradition, felt, though they
no longer dared to voice the opinion, that after all there was something indecently utilitarian about all these scientists. Of course, one
had to give them credit for the fact that they did not *mean* to be
utilitarian; they were seekers after knowledge for its own sake, but
there was always the chance that, by accident, they would stumble on
something *useful*, a cure or something equally vulgar. Now a classical
scholar could be relied upon never, under any circumstances, to do
anything that could conceivably be of *use*, though it might be of
interest. However, in the middle of the 19th century, they had
supposed that they had "to move with the times," and had, in
consequence, erected these brick rabbit warrens on a piece of slum-
property, at a decent distance from the *real* University. A decision
which had been strongly criticised by certain elderly gentlemen, who
had taken advantage of the occasion to point out that the University
drew a nice little revenue from the slum property, whereas all the new
buildings not only meant that they would lose this, but that they
would actually have to spend money.

These thoughts drifted idly through the professor's mind as he
poked his way methodically from dingy little room to dingy little
room, pausing to look at the photographs of cocks turned into hens,
bull-dog calves and the multi-coloured skins of budgerigars which
hung on the manure-tinted walls.

In a large, fairly well-lighted room he came across Peter Hatton,
seated at a bench under the window surrounded by milk-bottles, with
an inch of agar-agar in the bottom and stopped with plugs of cotton-
wool. Inside these bottles whole generations of the vinegar-fly, *drosophila melanogaster*, were breeding, spending their lives and dying,
while eager eyes watched for a variant of the wild type, a white or a
brown eye in place of the scarlet, or a notched or wrinkled wing.

Peter picked up one of these bottles and skilfully inverted it over a
jar, inside which there was a copper gauze funnel. He shook the flies
from their home into this and waited for a moment until the ether in
the cotton-wool at the bottom of the jar had taken effect, then he

tipped the anaesthetised drosophila out on to a sheet of glass and, with a camel-hair brush, selected one or two which he placed on a slide under a binocular microscope.

"Humph," said Professor Stubbs, "when did you see Dr. Swartz last?"

Peter, fiddling at his microscope, did not look up at the question. "Really," he said, "I suppose I should be wearing pale-blue silk and you should be a Roundhead. Actually I saw Swartz last night at the Gene-group meeting. He got up to leave at the same time as I did, about a quarter to ten. I had to leave before the end because I was meeting Mary, who'd been seeing a girl friend, and I might just as well have waited till the end, for she was nearly half an hour late. Why do you want to know about Swartz?"

With a steel-needle he centered a fly on the slide and applied his eyes again to the microscope. Professor Stubbs snorted, "Humph. He's disappeared and the police are on the lookout for him." He looked round the room and rumbled, "Lot of cupboards in here. Wonder what's in them." Peter continued to examine the flies while the professor stumped solemnly round the room, opening cupboards and looking into them inquisitively, replacing the things that his curiosity dislodged.

"What's in this?" he bellowed suddenly, and Peter turned round, startled, to see him pointing at a long narrow cupboard beside the door. "Oh, nothing much. I think it's the place where Fielding, whose room this is, keeps his overalls and so on."

The professor did not seem to be listening. He was leaning forward and examining the key-hole, which was blocked with a bright fragment of broken metal where someone had snapped the key in the lock. Straightening up, the professor stumped round the room, examining the benches with the air of one who does not quite know for what he is searching. His eyes fixed on a bunsen burner and he disconnected the rubber gas-pipe from the heavy metal base and picked it up by the thin brass neck and returned to the cupboard, swinging the burner in his hand like a man testing the weight of a hammer. He examined the lock and lifted the bunsen burner.

"Look here, sir," said Peter, anxiously, "you can't do that. This isn't my room. I've just borrowed it. We can't break up a man's room."

"Oh, can't I?" remarked the professor fiercely, and he smashed the burner down on the lock. Peter looked on, feeling very worried at this desecration of another man's property, while Professor Stubbs rained sledge-hammer blows on the lock, panting between them. "It shouldn't stand much of this... it's not a good lock... another two or three should do the trick...."

The door creaked faintly under the assault and he raised the bunsen burner and sighted carefully on the crack he had made beside the lock. The heavy base sunk into the opening for a distance of about a couple of inches and the professor leaned his weight upon it, using it as a lever. The wood groaned and then there was a sharp crack as the lock gave way, having proved unequal to the strain.

Puffing like a walrus, the professor stood back and laid his makeshift hammer down on the table. Slowly, ever so slowly, the door swung open, and a figure which had been crammed inside toppled forward. Peter jumped up to catch it, but the professor stood in his way, making no movement. The face of the figure was a dark purple in colour, but even if nothing else had been identifiable, Peter would have known it by the empty corn-cob pipe clenched tightly in the set teeth. The body of Herman Swartz thudded to the ground and still the professor made no other movement than to take his pipe out of his pocket and start to scrape it methodically.

CHAPTER 3

───────────

CALICO PIE

Neither of them said anything for a full minute. The silence seemed the deeper for the sound of the professor's penknife scraping away the clotted carbon on the bowl of his pipe. As he scratched a match between his finger-nails to light it, it sounded like the breaking down of a vast machine. He sighed, "Well, when Inspector Hargrave said he'd gone I was afraid of this. I don't see what I could have done to prevent it. Peter." The young doctor jumped smartly to attention at the parade ground sergeant-major roar. "Will you go and phone the inspector and tell him what we've found? I'll wait here till you come back. Don't use the janitor's phone but go across to the common-room and use one of the boxes, and don't mention it to anyone, not even to Mary."

Glad of the excuse to leave the room, Peter tilted his flies back into their bottle and corked them up with a fresh wad of cotton-wool. "I won't be long, sir," he said and closed the door gently behind him. Alone, the professor bent down over the body of Swartz and, removing his pipe, sniffed at his mouth. He screwed up his face in distaste and murmured to himself. "Cyanide again. The damn' fool." Feeling through his pockets he unearthed a powerful magnifying glass and, grinning a little to himself at the thought of playing Sherlock Holmes or Dr. Thorndyke, he examined the skin about the nose and the upper lip and found it slightly abrased. "Hmm," he grunted and replaced his glass in his pocket, "I thought as much. Oh, the devil—and all so unnecessary."

He straightened up again and relit his pipe, which had gone out. Looking down at the body he sighed and mumbled, "What? Frightened by false fire?" Then he recommenced his peering round the room, looking anxiously at the bottles with their families of red-eyed flies as if imploring them to speak and tell him what had happened in the room.

The door opened quietly and the professor turned to face it. The eager face of Professor Silver appeared with the cockatoo lock of hair dangling over his forehead. He grinned at Professor Stubbs in a friendly manner, "Dr. Fielding not in? How are you this morning? I've just sent the corrected proofs of my book back to my publishers and felt that I could do with a little entertainment. Fielding told me that he'd come across some inexplicable things in a wild population of *drosophila sub-obscura* and invited me to drop in some time."

His harsh voice was as disturbing as the croaking of frogs on a summer's night and Professor Stubbs said nothing. He seemed to be listening to something with his head cocked on one side. Silver did not seem to be the least put out by his inattention but advanced further into the room and the door, worked by a spring, closed slowly behind him, disclosing the body of Swartz lying on the floor.

Silver stared at the body for a moment and then screeched, "God, what's happened to Swartz? He's dead—dead like Ian." He looked across at Professor Stubbs and his eyes narrowed and his eyebrows seemed to meet in a straight line. "What do you know about this?" His grating voice was crafty and he took a step forward towards the professor, who remained silent and as still as the Bass Rock. Silver looked down at Swartz once more and then turned towards Professor Stubbs, his voice breaking as he screamed, "You murdered him and you murdered Ian. You swine! You can't get away with it, you won't get away with it."

While he was speaking his feet were slithering over the floor and, as he finished, he jumped awkwardly at the professor, who stuck out a short thick arm and pushed him over bellowing, "Don't be a bloody fool, man." Silver collapsed like a punctured motor-tyre and sat down on a low stool, covering his face with his hands. For a moment or two he sobbed dryly and then, opening his fingers, he glanced up at Professor Stubbs suspiciously. The professor did not seem to be paying much attention to him but was still looking down at Swartz with a strange, quizzical smile twisting his usually cheerful face.

He swung his bulk round to face Silver and roared, "Stopped being a damned fool, eh? You know as well as I do that I have had no hand in either of these murders. It doesn't do anybody any good to have you throwin' hysterical fits." His voice dropped to a low rumble. "I think I've got a pretty fair idea of the murderer and, while I might have had some doubts about helping to hang anyone for the murder of Porter, who was askin' to be murdered anyhow, I'll have no scruples about helpin' to hang that same person as high as Haman for the murder of Swartz. The first murder was excusable, but this is not. A dog can have one bite by law, and though we may disapprove publicly of its bitin' we may be quite pleased secretly because it has bitten someone we all dislike, but when that dog bites someone we like we demand that it be muzzled, at the least. I know who murdered Porter and Swartz and I'm goin' to prove my case."

Silver stood up and spoke harshly. "I don't think you can expect me to agree with your estimate of poor Ian. I know a lot of people didn't like him, but then a lot of people who are jealous of someone who is cleverer and more successful than they are themselves hide their jealousy by pretending that they do not like that person as a man. If ever a man suffered from this, Ian did. He knew exactly what he wanted and that is something so rare that when they encounter it people are frightened as well as jealous. They accused him of stealing the ideas of better men when he suggested some line of work to someone and then carried it to a successful conclusion after the other had failed. Was that stealing? No, I tell you. He was taking what was rightfully his, and no one could disprove his claims to his own property. I was his best friend and we worked together for a long time, and not once during that period did I find him trying to take more than his share of the credit for any line of work. I tell you that and I should know if anyone knows."

Professor Stubbs sucked on his pipe and spoke quietly. "Don't you think, Silver, that we've had about enough of this attempted white-washin' of the late Dr. Porter? You know that his reputation was, as the sayin' is, none too savoury, and he did nothin' to redeem it by bein' murdered. You know that he stole from you as he stole from everyone else with whom he came in contact. I won't weep any tears over Porter—if I did they would be crocodile's tears, whatever these may be. But Swartz was one of my friends and I don't like losin' my friends in this way. I don't like it at all. In fact, I may tell you that I feel quite revengeful about it, and I'm not a man who's much given to feelin' that way. I am goin' to see that the neck of the person who murdered Swartz is snapped if I have to do it myself."

Silver sneered, "Oh yes, Stubbs, we all know you'd make a great detective. It's about the only thing you haven't tried. You'll tire of it fairly soon, though, just as you've tired of everything else. You are always the potentially brilliant man who would do something really great if he was not so lazy! Laziness covers a multitude of sins, and in your case you hide your lack of originality behind the excuse of 'can't be bothered.' Go ahead then, playing at being a hero with a cloak and swordstick, and then when you find yourself stuck you can always say you couldn't summon up enough energy to find the evidence you wanted, but that you know the murderer, and you'll wrap the name of the murderer up in swaddling clothes of mystery so that none but yourself will know who it is you mean and only a few will realise that you have not the slightest idea of the murderer's identity, but are merely playing mystery-man."

Looking at Silver over the tops of his glasses, Professor Stubbs half-closed his eyes as he replied, "You know, Silver, there's a good deal of truth in what you say. I didn't realise that you knew me so well." He laughed softly and swung round towards the door, which had opened once more to admit Peter.

"They shouldn't be long, Professor Stubbs," he said, keeping his eyes steadfastly turned from the body on the floor. "The inspector said we weren't to touch it." He paused, gazing at Silver. "Pretty ghastly, isn't it? First Porter and then poor old Swartz, who was a damned decent fellow and pretty clever. I'd like to get my fingers on the swine that did it."

Silver nodded and grated, "So would I." He looked down at his thin arms and added, "Not that I could do much if I did find him."

There was silence in the room for several minutes after this, no one appearing anxious to leave in case the police put some interpretation upon their departure and wish to escape being interviewed. Professor Stubbs stood beside the body of Swartz, blowing clouds of smoke from his pipe and rocking backwards and forwards on his heels. On his stool Silver sat, pulling letters out of his pockets, reading them and replacing them, while Peter sat down at his microscope and made some pretence of examining a dead fly which he found near the window-sill, moving it about on the slide carefully with his steel needle.

The inspector's lips were closed in a tight line as he examined the body of Dr. Swartz and then made room for his assistants and for Dr. Flanagan. He looked at Professor Stubbs sharply, "You found him, did you, Professor? Well, I'll deal with these others first, and then I'll hear what you have to say." He fixed his eyes pointedly upon the broken lock of the cupboard, and then beckoned Peter to follow him down to the far end of the room, out of earshot of the others.

"Dr. Hatton, have you been working here all morning? Yes? Yet you never thought of looking into that cupboard. Did you notice that someone had snapped the key off short in the lock? No? Don't you think that's strange?"

With the air of one about to explain the mysteries of life to a child, Peter answered him very gently. "I don't think it the least strange, inspector. This is not my room and was merely lent to me to do some work. I have been here before and I know that the owner of this room, Dr. Fielding, keeps his overall and an old jacket in that cupboard. I don't know about you, Inspector Hargrave, but when I find myself alone in a friend's room I am not in the habit of looking into their private drawers and cupboards, nor do I feel inclined to rifle the pockets of any jackets or coats that they leave lying about. Of course, if I was a policeman I might behave in a different way, but then I don't know whether policemen carry their public manners into their private lives."

Inspector Hargrave's lips tightened even more than before and white lines appeared on his cheeks at the corner of his mouth. Opening his lips to the extent of a narrow slit, he ground out, "Dr. Hatton, I must ask you to treat my questions seriously. I do not suppose that I need to remind you that I am only doing my duty."

"All right, old cock," replied Peter cheerfully, "I'll try to answer your questions if you'll try not to be so damned offensive. I resented your innuendo that I was in the habit of poking into things that do not concern me. No, I noticed nothing out of the ordinary in here, but then I wouldn't in any case, as this is not my room. The person to ask about that is Dr. Fielding."

"When did you see Dr. Swartz last and did his behaviour strike you as being perfectly normal?"

Resisting the temptation to say that he had last seen Swartz a few moments previously and that he had looked anything but normal,

Peter answered him seriously, "At about a quarter to ten last night. I was at a meeting and he was there. When I saw him rise to go before the end, I looked at my watch and saw that it was time that I too left. I walked along the corridor with him, and we spoke about the meeting we had just attended. Now I come to think of it, I suppose he was rather more excited than he usually appeared, but I suppose I put that down to the fact that it had been a very good meeting and several people had made suggestions which might repay further investigation and I assumed, that just as I had, he had thought of something he wanted to try out. I left him at the cloak-room, as I wanted to brush my hair before my appointment. Yes, I suppose he must have had an appointment with someone, but he didn't say anything to me about it. Is that all right?"

The inspector nodded his head vaguely and said, "That'll do for the present, but I may need to ask you a few questions later on and I hope you'll hold yourself in readiness to answer them. You can go now. No, I'm sorry, but this room will have to be kept locked until we've finished with it, so you'll need to do your work somewhere else. Yes, I'll tell the officer in charge that you have my permission to come in and collect any odds and ends you need when you've found another place in which to work. You'll show him what you're taking and give him a list of them, won't you? That's all, thank you, doctor."

Peter wandered down the room and spoke to Professor Stubbs, "We're all for it. That inspector chap doesn't believe anything we say. We're all to hold ourselves in readiness for further questioning." He mimicked the inspector's tone. The professor grunted and his eyes twinkled. "We've found his murder suspect and now he's been murdered. Don't be too hard on him. He must be beginnin' to wonder whether he's the leader or the tail-end of a Caucus race."

Silver's voice was jarring away at the far end of the room, like a broken gramophone record. "I just came in a few minutes ago, looking for Dr. Fielding. The last time I saw Dr. Swartz was, as far as I remember, about lunch-time yesterday. I spent the afternoon and evening in my room in the hostel, correcting the proofs of a book."

The inspector leaned forward. "So that's all you know, Professor Silver?" Silver snarled spitefully, "I'm not pretending to give you advice, inspector, but don't you think that Stubbs there knows too much about this murder? He's very dramatic about it, saying Swartz was a friend of his, but I noticed that he did not worry much about the death of Ian Porter, of whom he was jealous."

In his mind, Inspector Hargrave toned down the snarl, discounting most of it as personal spite, but he made a reservation that it did seem a little bit odd that the professor should know so much about the hiding place of Swartz's body. He dismissed Silver abruptly, warning him that he might be needed again and asking him to find Dr. Fielding if possible; then he called to the professor, who came stumping across the room, beaming genially.

"You will understand, Professor," the opening was tentative, "that I have to satisfy both my private inquisitiveness and my official curiosity. I want you, if you don't mind, to tell me exactly how you came to find Dr. Swartz's body and what, in the first place, made you start looking for him. All the information we had this morning was that he had disappeared and that the evidence, for which you yourself were largely responsible, pointed to him as the killer of Dr. Porter."

The professor gave a hoot like a startled owl. "My dear fellow, I told you last night that I could make out as good a case against myself if you wanted to hear it. I was merely tryin' to show you that anyone of us could have committed the murder while Andrew Blake was incapable of it. I did not mean you to suspect Swartz, for I did not think that he had killed Porter, though his motive was undoubtedly the most direct and the easiest for the ordinary person to understand. I chose him merely as an example, because I could make a fairly convincin' case out of my head. Convincin', that is, provided you do not look at it too closely.

"When you told me this morning that Swartz had disappeared, I, realisin' that he was not the murderer, was immediately afraid that somethin' had happened to him, for, in addition, I knew that he had some clue as to the identity of the murderer. He didn't tell me but you only had to look at him to see that he was nursin' some secret, and it didn't seem to be likely that it was about anythin' else. If he knew the murderer, or somethin' about him and the murderer knew this, well, it looked as though he might have got into trouble of some sort.

"When you look at the murder of Porter you will see that really it is not an extremely original method; what makes it look so is that the stage settin', chosen mostly for its convenience, is strange. I had my doubts as to whether the murderer would have sufficient brains to change his method and so, acting on the assumption that only the immediate stage-settin' would be different, I started to look in case he had managed to murder Dr. Swartz. When I came into this room and saw that a key had been neatly snapped off in the lock of that cupboard, I was suspicious, as I don't like coincidences, and so I smashed the door open with the butt-end of a bunsen burner."

The inspector did not seem to be very satisfied with this up-the-airy-mountain description of Professor Stubbs' adventures in detection, but he was forced to be content with it, for the professor, ignoring his gesture of the lifted hand, was strolling back to where the doctor was at work on Swartz's body. "Same old poison, Joe," he boomed, "how was it done this time?"

Dr. Flanagan turned his head. "You old scoundrel," he remarked amicably, "I'd be willing to bet that, so far as we can tell without a post-mortem, you know as much about it as I do. Come on, now, give us a lecture on how the poison was administered."

With suspicious readiness, Professor Stubbs started, in a rumbling undertone that gradually grew to a roar. "All right, Joe, you've asked for it. I'll tell you what I think happened. The murderer, havin' decided that Swartz would have to be removed, made an appointment with him in this room. The reason that Swartz would have to be eliminated was obviously that he knew, or nearly knew, who the murderer was, and so there was no doubt that he would be suspicious. Swartz would not be likely to sit down on a chair to have a drop of blood drawn from his ear, for that, I think, was what the original plan required from Porter, so some other method of pacifying him had to be found.

"If you will look around this room, sooner or later your eye will come to rest on a vast bottle, with a prominent label, 'Ether.' No doubt our friend the murderer, lookin' round this room, noted the bottle and made plans accordingly. Now if you look at the electric light switch you will see that it is not in the usual place, but about six feet along the wall.

"Think, gentlemen, for a moment. You come into a dark room, or a room which has been darkened by the use of these convenient close-fittin' black blinds, and you feel for the electric light switch, runnin' your hand along the wall until you find it. All this time you keep your body pressed against the wall, as you cannot help being afraid of trippin' over somethin', particularly if you know you are in someone's workroom, and that one breakage may result in the destruction of several years' work.

"The murderer realised this and the plans were laid accordingly. I think that the murderer came up here some time before Swartz was due, and set the stage, placin', let us say, a stool here, where it was far enough inside the room to be invisible in the weak light filtered from the passage."

He walked heavily across the room and picked up one of the bench stools and placed it carefully, about three feet to the side of the door, and about two and a half feet from the wall.

"Then the murderer soaks a large pad in ether and sits down to wait for the steps in the passage that will act as a warnin' of the victim's approach. When the distant patter of the footsteps is heard—you have all noticed how your own steps echo in these corridors?—the murderer prepares and mounts the stool, probably quite calmly, as by this time the terrors will have passed and their place been taken by an icy determination to see the affair through, as Swartz's death appears to be an absolute necessity.

"Swartz enters the room and the change from even the faint light of the passage to the complete darkness of the room bewilders him for a moment. Remember, he is suspicious, but in the belief that the poisoner rarely resorts to violence and hearin' nothin', he pulls himself together and runs his hand around the wall in search of the electric light switch, moving further and further from the door. The murderer, with eyes accustomed to the dark, can see him clearly against the light. When his back is fully turned he suddenly feels two arms close round his neck and the throttling pad pressed over his mouth and nose.

"Naturally, he struggles with all his strength, and he was no weaklin', but his opponent has the advantage of havin' taken him both by surprise and from the back, and until you are attacked from behind by someone who is determined to kill you, you can have no idea how difficult it is to dislodge your unwelcome passenger. Imagine the struggle with Swartz fightin' for his life, in a frantic panic, while that pad is continually pressed over his nose and mouth and those beastly sickly fumes are chokin' him. I don't think that it was altogether the ether, but probably a combination of that and suffocation, but eventually Swartz would cease from strugglin' and would become unconscious. Then the murderer would, no doubt, pour more ether on the pad and finish the job of anaesthetisin' his victim. Do you agree with me, Joe? I think this will agree with the condition of the nose and mouth, don't you?"

The little doctor bent down again and pointed out the roughening of the skin to the police officers, remarking, "I don't think there's much doubt that it happened some way like that." The inspector nodded wisely, and Professor Stubbs held up his hand to show that he wished to get on with his lecture.

"I have already pointed out that our murderer is not a very original person, but merely works on the stage settin' or if you prefer it, on a large canvas, where the details are slashed in after the main outline, without very much regard as to whether they are pertinent or not. The murderer had cyanide and was determined to use it whether it was necessary or not, and here all that was needed was to batter poor Swartz over the head with one of these stools.

"Swartz was lyin' there unconscious and the murderer wished to pour poison into him. If you look around this room again you will see that there are plenty of funnels that would do the job admirably, but no, that is too simple for our murderer who is, we may say, the possessor of a perverted sense of humour. When you think of Swartz the first thing you remember is that corn-cob pipe which was never used for its natural purpose—for smokin'—but which was just something to chew. That was the thing the murderer remembered and it seemed to be a good idea to use the corn-cob as a funnel, so it was carefully inserted in Swartz's mouth and the cyanide was poured down it.

"Then our pleasant little friend shoved the body in that cupboard, locked the door and snapped off the key and probably went home to a good night's rest, in the fond belief that something attempted something done had, indeed, earned a night's repose. That, gentlemen, is roughly what I believe to have happened in this room at about ten o'clock last night."

He stood looking at the men in a semi-circle round him, as if waiting for contradiction or emendation of his theory, but no one said anything, though one or two heads nodded like those of *papier-mâché* mandarins. After a moment the Professor went to the door and opened it.

Inspector Hargrave suddenly came to life and leaped after him. "Excuse me, Professor, I'm sorry I forgot to ask you before, but, just as a matter of form, will you tell me what you did after you left me last night?"

Professor Stubbs looked at him and roared with laughter. "Well," and his voice boomed like Jeremiah Clarke's trumpet voluntary in an empty chapel, "if you must know, I went on a pub crawl to clear my brain."

CHAPTER 4

THE LITTLE BIRDS FLY

INSPECTOR HARGRAVE looked fixedly at the door which slammed behind the Professor. Dr. Flanagan, with the twinkling of steel instruments, stowed away his odds and ends in one of those bags only used to-day by doctors and bowls players. He jerked his thumb over his shoulder and remarked, "You might as well go by what he tells you. It fits all the facts that I could have told you. John Stubbs is nobody's fool. You mayn't be able to follow him all the way but that's because he begins at the wrong end, or at least a different place from anyone else. He's the sort of man who starts at the top of the ladder and works his way down to the bottom rung and then finds another ladder and repeats the process. You can take it that the murderer tried to make the victim unconscious with ether, and that it was as much suffocation as the ether that caused the unconsciousness. The poison *was* administered by pouring it into the bowl of that corn-cob. Thank God I smoke Players and no humorist will be able to use one of them as a feeding tube. No, you can take it from me that the description you've just been given of the happenings in this room is as clear a one as you're likely to have unless the murderer breaks down and confesses."

The inspector glanced at him sharply. "Don't you think that perhaps our friend knows a little bit *too* much about the murder? I'm willing to admit that he's quite astute, but I don't believe in all this reconstruction stuff he's been doing. In fact, if he'd been here watching, or taking part, he'd have been able to give us this account, but why he should do it I don't know."

"The trouble about having the professor as murderer," Sergeant Jenkins put in tentatively, "is that we've been picking his brains all along and we are dependent upon him for nearly all we've got so far. He showed us that the case against young Blake wouldn't stand, and to do this, or so he says, showed us that Swartz might be the guilty man. Then, while we're burning up the telephone wires, ringing Liverpool and Southampton, he hunts around and finds the body for us."

The inspector, surprised at his assistant's unusual verbosity, lifted his hand in a gesture of protest. "Of course," he said rather sulkily, "I wasn't suggesting that the professor was the murderer. After all, you, Jenkins, explored his alibi yourself for the murder of Porter and found that he could not have done it. All I said was that it was very funny that he should know so much about these murders."

The little doctor was chortling to himself. Inspector Hargrave looked at him suspiciously. "Oh no," exclaimed Dr. Flanagan, when he could control himself, "I've just had a mental picture of old John Stubbs perched on a stool with an ether-soaked pad waiting for his victim. No, I'm afraid you couldn't prove a very good case against him. Can't you imagine his counsel describing the professor stuck on top of that tiny stool, quivering like a jelly. Why, man, no one could possibly squeeze between his belly and the wall. You'd be laughed out of court."

The inspector's laughter held a grudging quality but he agreed with the doctor about the unlikeliness of Professor Stubbs having managed to do the murder, at any rate in the way which he had suggested it had been done. But he still clung to his point that he did not approve of too much knowledge of murder cases by mere spectators.

Professor Stubbs, unaware, or at least seemingly unaware of the fact that, for a few moments, the cloak of suspicion had fallen from Swartz's spare shoulders upon his own ample back, was sitting in the common-room with his papers spread out in front of him. He was making notes furiously upon the margins of an abstract from one of the genetical periodicals. As he wrote he swore to himself in what he fondly believed to be an undertone, with the result that he received some shocked looks from extremely respectable looking delegates and their wives.

He got to his feet at last, still with an occupied look on his face, so that he did not notice when he sent his coffee cup spinning to the floor to smash on the parquetry. "Hmm," he grumbled, like a bear irritated by a wasp, "I suppose I must be wrong, but I don't see where I've gone off the rails. Better suggest that they look into it."

Completely oblivious of the astonished glances which greeted his angry monologue, he continued through the room, steering his way between the tables without appearing to notice them. Standing in the hall, he tangled his grey mop of hair with one hand while with the other he shoved the sheaf of papers he carried into his jacket pocket and, with a continuance of the same movement, dug out his short black pipe, like a tinker's much-smoked clay.

He tapped the pipe out against the heel of his shoe and scraped it carefully with the little pearl-handled pen-knife which he carried, for that purpose only, in his waistcoat pocket. All the time he scraped at the carbon-lined bowl his lips were moving mechanically as he muttered to himself. His forehead was wrinkled and his eyes seemed to be following every movement of his blunt square-tipped fingers, as they took the piece of dark brown plug out of his waistcoat pocket and held it expertly for the shredding movements of the knife.

Slowly he crossed the little lawn that separated the common-room building from the rest of the brick buildings that made up the scientific side of the university. Entering the hall he saw Silver, rather like a marmoset, chattering away to several people. He nodded his large head in a gesture of recognition but ignored the unspoken invitation, conveyed by a slight widening of the circle, to join the gossipers.

As he walked along the stone corridors he noted the echoing thuds of his steps, like the slow tolling of a muffled bell, or the drums at a soldier's funeral and, in spite of himself, shivered slightly; his huge bulk jerking like a giant tree which has just received the final blow, the blow that leaves it ready for the crowbars to finish its crash to the damp fern-sprouting ground of the forest. Just so, he thought, the thud of Swartz approaching must have sounded to the murderer, perched on the stool beside the door.

He shook himself and growled gruffly. Striking a fusee between his finger nails he paused until the violent sulphurous fumes had abated and lit his pipe. Then, almost briskly he continued along the corridors, turning now to the left and now to the right, with the determination of a man who had made up his mind and who was intent on one purpose only.

At the door of Dr. Fielding's room he paused, almost imperceptibly, before knocking, arranging his words in advance. The door swung open an inch or two and a nose, ridden astride by two eyes, poked out through it, and inquired, "Wotyerwont" all as one word, before it recognised the Professor. Then it disappeared and a wrinkle of blue serge, a policeman's back, filled the opening and muffled, just about as much as a bowler hat mutes Louis Armstrong's trumpet, his voice as he shouted, "Professor Stubbs here, Inspector. Will I let him in?"

The reply was inaudible, but must have been favourable, for the door opened wide and the professor had a momentary vision of red felt, an awning and handfuls of confetti as the sergeant stood at attention to let him pass. Professor Stubbs stumped solemnly up the room to the far end, where Inspector Hargrave was in conference with Dr. Flanagan. The inspector, having cleared away a few of the milk bottles of vinegar-flies, was leaning on the edge of the bench smoking a cigarette, which he held between bunched fingertips with the lighted end towards the palm of his hand. He looked along his shoulder at Professor Stubbs. "Well, well, Professor, have you come to tell us who the murderer is and when he'll be murdered by someone else?" He laughed heartily at his own joke until, having forgotten that he was smoking a cigarette, a drift of smoke inflamed his eyes and started him coughing.

Professor Stubbs, unperturbed by the jeer or the coughing, continued to swathe his own head in thick rank clouds, until the Inspector had finished coughing and was once more leaning against the bench, with his eyes streaming. Then he spoke, "Look here, Inspector, I wonder whether you could do one thing for me? Find out if there are any witnesses to Silver's accounts of his occupation at the rough time of the murders. Oh, I know you more or less cleared him at the beginnin', but we certainly gave him rather a long time to go to his hostel and to find his paper—allowin' him about 23 minutes, from the time the janitor heard him goin' off for lunch until the time he was seen leavin' the hostel. I think we can rely on the janitor havin' the right time as the large electric clock in the hall is controlled by a master-clock and could not go wrong, and, remember, he was late for his lunch—havin' been held up by a phone call and would certainly be keepin' his eye on the clock. If, say, he did not leave the buildin' completely but returned by one of the other doors and found that, instead of havin' to make some excuse to Porter for postponin' his message, that his predestined victim was knocked out ready for him."

While he was speaking Professor Stubbs lumbered heavily up and down the room, with his hands clasped behind his back, under the tails of his jacket.

"I don't believe that Silver did either of these murders but I would just like to be convinced that it was impossible for him to have done them. You see, the plannin' of the first murder depended, as I have pointed out before, upon the murderer bein' sufficiently intimate with Porter to offer to take a drop of blood from his ear. The fact that Dr. Hatton's fist made this subterfuge unnecessary is a pure accident and we need not alter our ideas of the method because of it. Well, when you look at the case, one of the first things that strikes you is that undoubtedly Silver would have the best opportunity to do the murder as planned.

"Oh, yes, I know that Silver was Porter's best friend, but just because of that he may have had a very strong motive for murderin' him, or one that, at least, appeared very strong. He may have finally become exasperated at Porter's magpie habit of pickin' up his best ideas and have come to the conclusion that the death of Porter would be the only way to stop this stealin'. You don't think that a very strong motive, Inspector? Hmm, murders have often been committed for motives infinitely less strong than that. You, as a police officer, should realise that the strength of motive has very little to do with the gravity of the crime. Still, I told you, I don't think that Silver is our murderer, but before I can get my ideas properly focused on the real culprit, I must know that it was impossible for him to have done it."

The inspector chortled softly to himself. "Good old Sherlock," he said offensively, "you are never beaten, are you? You'll still be finding us murderers when the real one is hanging from the gallows. You know, Professor, you are bound to find the right murderer in the end for you are carefully proving how each person did the murder. The only trouble about your system is that having found your murderer you then go on to show that he couldn't have done it in spite of the seemingly strong case against him. If only you'd leave your case half way and just show me why someone had done the murder I'd be grateful. I could have brought quite a good case against young Blake or Swartz here," he gestured with his thumb at the place where the body had been, a chalk outline on the floor.

Chuckling wickedly, Professor Stubbs rumbled heavily, "So ho, Inspector, you think you can get a murderer—do you? Well, I'll give you a word of warnin'—I know who did this murder, though I'm not in a position to prove it at the moment and if you get the wrong person, why, damn it man, I'll instruct the defence myself and blow your case as high as the Eiffel Tower and make you look an even bigger fool than you are by nature, difficult though that may be. If you'd half as much sense as you should have, you'd have as much idea of the murderer as I have and you've got so many better opportunities of proving a case. I'll give you a hint, since you're lost, go to the public library and look along the *Notable Trials Series*. You'll find your answer pat in one of these, motive and all the rest of it."

He laughed and Inspector Hargrave who had been scowling heavily, followed his example after a moment. "No offence, Inspector?" the professor inquired breezily. "No? That's good. I was just bein' forcible. Now, will you do what I ask? Just find out how complete Silver's alibis are for the times of the murders. I would feel more comfortable if I knew that it was absolutely impossible for Professor Silver to have done the murder. Then when I produce my murderer from my pocket you won't be able to bring him up as a red herrin' to prove that I am wrong. You see I want to make certain before I start throwin' my accusations about. Oh, by the way, you impounded the papers that were lyin' about in the demonstration-room, didn't you? I wonder whether I could have a look at them. There might be somethin' there that we have missed."

The inspector laughed good-naturedly, "Oh, very well, if it amuses you, you can have a look at them, though I warn you that I've already chewed them over pretty carefully and there's nothing to them. They're just variations in people's tastes. Dr. Swartz explained them to me. Sergeant Jenkins is going back to headquarters now. If you care to go with him I'll give you a chit to say that you can have access to the papers, and I hope they'll do you some good."

He tore a sheet of paper from his notebook and, wetting the point of his pencil between pouted lips, scribbled rapidly on it, folded it up into a pellet and handed it to Professor Stubbs, who took it with the air of being grateful for small mercies, and stuffed it carefully into one of his waistcoat pockets. Followed by Sergeant Jenkins he stumped solidly out of the door.

Turning to Dr. Flanagan, Inspector Hargrave laughed, "I'm afraid, Doc, that your old pal is more than a little bit of a fraud. He knows that I have been making use of the fact that he is at home among these people, in the hope of getting a proper lead from his knowledge of them and their surroundings. That, with too much Edgar Wallace, seems to have gone to his head and he imagines that he is the great detective, complete with bags of mystery. It is all very well for these story book detectives to point out that the police are blunderers, but in real life you'll find that we get much further by sheer hard work, than we would if we lay back in our chairs and used our 'little grey cells.' When we get the murderer we'll do it by eliminating everyone else and you can't do that by psychology or magic, but just by sheer hard work. Why, you'll notice that whenever he wants any real work done he comes to us and asks us to do it. I may tell you that the only reason that we do it is because he usually suggests lines which we have already marked out for further investigation, and it doesn't make much difference what order we do them in. One line appears as likely to give us a clue as another."

The little doctor lit a cigarette carefully and flicked out the match before he replied. "Oh, yes. I know John Stubbs is a charlatan, but he's a charlatan of an odd sort. He likes to appear as a miracle worker, who can produce the pigeon from a top hat off a stranger's head, but to do this he puts in a lot of hard work previously, following the stranger round until he can exchange hats so skilfully that the victim will not know of the trick which has been played upon him. He's a stage magician, only a wizard if you don't know of all the paraphernalia hidden behind the scenes. Besides, you yourself must admit that you haven't got a line on the murderer yet, and it doesn't seem likely that you'll get one before this congress finishes and if you don't you'll find your job much harder, for at present you've only got to pick your choice out of a covey, but a week from now your birds will be scattered all over

the field! When John Stubbs says he knows the murderer you may be
pretty sure that he really has some idea that is worth something. If I
was in your position, Inspector, knowing so little, I'd play along with
him as being one of your only chances. Like the famous Sherlock, I
dare say there is some method in his madness. Even if it only
succeeds in clarifying matters you will have gained a few points on
your present position."

The inspector muttered that the professor was too damn' clever by
half and was putting up suspects like Aunt Sallies, and then knocking
them down, so as to protect himself if he was proved wrong. Then he
brightened and remarked that, if they could break his alibi, Professor
Silver was as good a suspect as any he had come across. He invited the
doctor to lunch with him as soon as he had made his report and they
left the room, locking it behind them, empty but for the hundreds of
flies madly breeding and dying, white eyes, red eyes, brown eyes,
wings twisted, notched and shortened so as to be useless for flight, in
milk bottles with an inch of agar-agar, each bottle a self sufficient
nationalist state, permitting no intercourse with its neighbours.

In the inspector's cubby-hole of an office Professor Stubbs sat,
overflowing from the official chair, with various papers spread out in
front of him. With a complete disregard for the taxpayer's pocket he
was copying certain of these papers out at length on the official paper
provided for the inspector, which he had run to earth in one of the
desk drawers.

He carefully ruled sheets of paper so as to duplicate the tasting
sheets and filled them in painfully and checked them to make certain
that he had exactly copied the originals.

Everytime he leaned over the desk it seemed to be on the point of
upsetting, but just in time it rocked back on to four legs.

When the inspector arrived back, followed by Dr. Flanagan, the
professor was leaning back in the chair with his eyes shut and smoke
pouring from the pipe hidden in his moustache. This smoke was so
thick that it was all that the inspector could do to make out the vast
buddha-like figure occupying his chair.

Holding his breath the inspector advanced through balls of discarded
paper and flung open the window and turned to waken the sleeper
who, however, was watching him. "Ah ha, fresh-air fiend, I see," he
remarked. "I like fresh air as well as the next one, but I like mine out
of doors, not in a room. I come into a room to get away from fresh air,
I don't invite it in with me."

He swung a heavy leg from the corner of the desk where it had
been resting, spilling a box of paper clips and pen-nibs, and straight-

ened up slowly. "Well, I've copied out all that I want. Now I'll need to see what good it is. Thanks for the loan of the room."

He lumbered out, leaving an irritated inspector, who as a stickler for tidiness felt rather ill-treated, to fan the smoke through the window, pick up the balls of paper and the paper clips, and generally attempt to restore some sort of order to the devastated office.

PART THREE

HERE COMES THE BOGY

I NEVER FELT SO PLEASED in all my life as I did that morning
when they let me out of jail. I had been feeling a rope around my neck
the whole night and it certainly was not a pleasant feeling. Lying on
the narrow bunk which did duty as a bed, I had almost succeeded in
persuading myself that I had, indeed, murdered Porter and had then
forgotten all about it. This may sound absurd and I can't say that I
really expect anyone who reads this to believe me, but all the same it
is true and it worried me a great deal.

Though I was very sorry to hear that Swartz had also been murdered,
in one way it made things easier for me, for I had an absolutely
unbreakable alibi, with half the local policemen as my witnesses, and
not even the most determined prosecutor could have attempted to
break it down. There were no convenient secret passages from the
cell. If there had been I would have found them, for I spent quite a bit
of the evening walking around thumping the walls in an absent-
minded way. There was an elderly, stout police-officer who was going
bald, so that all he retained of his hair was a black skull cap and it
reminded me painfully of that little piece of mediaeval pageantry, the
judge's black cap. Altogether I spent rather an unpleasant time and
made up my mind that I would not visit one of these places again,
even under the mild charges of D. and D. or D. and I., which initials
stand, for those who know, for the mystical after-the-party Drunk and
Disorderly, or Drunk and Incapable.

When I encountered the *Daily Courier* reporter he seemed sorry to
see me, for he had just written up a good story about me and would
need to scrap it, besides all the build-up he was planning which was to
carry me through the trial and on to the very trap of the gallows.

Personally, I thought his regrets for my innocence were just a trifle ghoulish, and, in consequence, I was rather short with him and refused to give him the low-down on my imprisonment and release.

The morning passed quickly enough, for, although Peter told me that Swartz had been murdered, I had to do some catching up on my articles for the paper and got more about his pet flies from him than about the murder. I did not want to get mixed up in the murder myself as I had come to the conclusion that one per week was quite sufficient for the Blake stomach, which was not strong at the best of times and preferred its blood and mystery between old calf covers or original blue boards, with a printed label on the back.

When I had scribbled off something about the family of *drosophila* and its super-rabbit habits in the way of breeding (when I was at school I once had a family of white mice that ran them pretty close; I note this in the interests of science), I went to look for my Uncle as he had told me that he would buy me lunch to restore my shattered nerves. The janitor, apparently sharing the general disappointment at my release, informed me that Professor Stubbs had left a message that I was to meet him at the police station.

I wondered vaguely what mischief he had been up to, and departed, thinking that it was pretty tactless of him to arrange to meet me at a place of which I had so very few pleasant memories.

As I drew near to the police station I heard a familiar voice roaring like a blowing whale, and turning a corner I saw my Uncle in violent argument with a couple of policemen. "So this is a one-way street, is it?" he was shouting, "well, why the hell didn't you say so or have a notice stuck up. Oh, there is a notice? Well, you should have a larger one. I thought that was an advertisement for cigarettes or a fish and chip shop or somethin' of the sort."

I edged my way through the crowd which had gathered to watch the battle and he saw me and gestured to me to get into the car, which was shaking as if nearly as indignant as its owner. "All right, have it your own way," he boomed and the gears crashed violently. People scattered away from us on all sides as the car started to snake backwards down the street at about thirty miles an hour.

By the time we reached the main road my Uncle had had time to accelerate to nearly 40 m.p.h. so that we were traveling fairly fast when we hit, or nearly hit, the main stream of traffic. Uncle John paid no attention to the expletives from other road users which descended upon his ample shoulders like confetti, but slammed home the gears and, neatly placing the Bentley between a horse-drawn coal-cart and an empty hearse, shot into a side street. Conversation being impossible, I contented myself with the thought that the hearse was following us and concentrated upon trying to move ten-ton lorries out of the way by the use of will-power and a hypnotic eye. I must admit, in all fairness to his driving that, awful driver that he is, I have never seen him drive worse and I am convinced that the only reason that we did not have an accident was that he never envisaged the possibility of such a thing and his faith carried him through, under the startled and unappreciative eyes of policemen who had not time to move before he was gone.

The car was, if I may use the phrase, thrown on its haunches as he stopped it outside a public-house called *The Swan in the Sand*. I lay back in the seat and closed my eyes in an attempt to recover my breath and to give my cheeks, which I guessed would be about the tone of a pale cheese, time to recover their normal tints.

When I felt that I was strong enough to stand on the ground without my knees clapping together like a pair of castanets my Uncle was already in the bar joking with the man who had filled two pint mugs and was engaged in expertly slicing roast beef to go beside the vast chunks of bread which lay like bergs on the white surface of the blue-edged plates. I suddenly realised that I was very hungry indeed and helped to carry the lunch over to an oak table in the corner. Uncle John picked up the glass mug and examined the amber beer against the light. "Here's the skin off your nose," he remarked gravely and tilted it to his lips. About half a pint slid down his gullet before he laid the mug down and wiped the fringe of froth from his moustache with the back of his hand.

He seemed to be engaged in some deep line of thought and did not speak to me as he ate his bread and beef. When it was finished he engulfed the rest of his beer, waited until I had done the same and picking up the mugs returned to the counter. He leaned over towards the barman and I heard him whisper the word "telephone." The barman pointed with a jerk of his thumb and my Uncle went through a glass door. He was not gone for long and when he returned his face had lightened.

"I've just been sendin' out invitations to a dinner party," he boomed across at me as he carried the beer over. "Tonight, my boy, you will eat in noble company. I've just left a message at the police station askin' Inspector Hargrave and Joe Flanagan to dinner to-night and I have promised them that I'll give them the murderer of Porter and Swartz. The sergeant who took my message did not seem to put much trust in my promise but said that he would deliver it all right.

"Now I've got a job for you to do for me. First," he dug out his wallet and gave me a note, "I want you to buy me a butterfly-net, or, better still, the largest size of landin' net you know, the sort of thin' used by trout fishermen, and, while you wait, have them fit it with a two-foot handle. What do I want it for? Ah ha, that's still to be seen but I'll tell you this, I always fancy that if I'd been put in an arena and given the choice of the trident and the net that I'd have put up a better show with a net. I want to give it a try out as I have no wish to lose my life helpin' the police. The other thing I want you to do is to go to the Western Union cable people's office and ask them if you can have a copy of any cable that arrived for Dr. Swartz, either care of the congress or at his hotel."

I suggested that the probability was that the Western Union would refuse to issue a copy of any cable to an unauthorised person like myself. He winked, contorting the whole of his face and drew a sheet of official police paper from his pocket. Upon this he wrote neatly, "Please provide bearer with copy of any cable addressed Swartz." He signed it with an illegible signature. "I don't think they'll question this," he rumbled, looking magnificently pleased with himself. "You look like one of those vast eunuch cats," I said coarsely, "just about ready to burst if anyone put butter on your toes."

He roared at me fiercely that I should hurry and do what he asked and remember that he was a busy man whose time was not to be wasted by the vulgar insults of urchins. When I left him he was scribbling a caricature of himself as a neuter tom on the back of one of his papers.

I had a bit of difficulty with the fishing tackle people where I went to buy the landing net. The man insisted upon telling me that for the size of net I was buying I would need a long handle so as to get sufficient leverage to lift the gargantuan fish I proposed to catch into the boat. I explained that I did not want it for catching ordinary fish and, shaking his head sadly, he retired to the back of the shop to exchange the long aluminium shaft for a short one meant to be used on a gaff. I am sure he charged me quite a lot more than he would have done if I had just bought the long-handled net, thinking that I might as well pay for my madness.

Rather to my surprise the girl in the Western Office made no difficulty about giving me a repeat of the cable for Dr. Swartz, though she showed an inclination to try and pump me about the murders, obviously under the impression that as I carried official paper I was a plain clothes detective and might give her some tit-bit of news that had not appeared in the paper, which she could make use of to impress her friends. Not knowing anything more than she did, I could not give her any information, but did my best to appear suitably mysterious so that she would feel that she had been visited by one of the very greatest of all detectives. Muttering something deep about Scotland Yard and Whitehall 1212, I left the office, sure that I was a great man in at least one place.

I looked at the cable but could make no sense of it and decided that it was in code. It began as follows: "Re P stop A3B2C4D1E3F2G1, etc." I hoped that my Uncle would be able to make more of it than I had.

Up at the University I found my uncle, who seemed to have an unlimited capacity for liquid, drinking tea with the colourless young man who had been Swartz's assistant in the tasting demonstration. When he saw me approaching Uncle John carefully folded up a piece of paper upon which he had been writing and shoved it into his pocket. The young man slammed a thick notebook shut and put it under his arm. When I got within earshot they were talking, with an appearance of the deepest interest, about the weather. I sat down and tried to join in this conversation, but after two or three minutes the game palled and I said, "What were you talking about when I came in?"

My uncle nodded his head wisely and his grey hair fell down over his forehead. He placed a thick finger against his nose, in a gesture made familiar by Fagan, and whispered, "Psst. I have a secret and I'm tryin' to find a way to stop it bein' a secret. Ask no questions and you'll be told no lies." He boomed suddenly, in a voice that penetrated the whole building, "Damn it all, can't you be patient and let an old man have his secrets to himself for a short time. I am Eagle Eye the detective, and Dogsnose the terror of the crooks, and between us I think I will solve the problem of the Duchess's jewels and the seven lumps of salt. You will find the essential clue lies in the pepper-pot filled with spider's eggs, but you must not forget the glass of chartreuse and the fly on the dial of the clock."

I saw that I would not get far and decided that I would need to wait until the evening before I got my answer. I handed my uncle the landing-net, which, wrapped in brown paper, looked rather like a tennis racket, and also the cable. He put the latter into his pocket without looking at it and tucked the net under his arm.

Looking at me fiercely he announced, "I've got to do some work now. I do not want to be disturbed and so I'm goin' back to the hotel to find some privacy. Do not interrupt me for any reason whatsoever. I will see you later."

He lumbered down the room, leaving me to pay for his tea and for the tea of the dim young man who had said nothing. I tried to talk to him but he could not think of anything to say except that he did not know how he would ever get over the death of Swartz. I dare say I was slightly unkind, but I felt that I could not stand the thin voice dribbling away mournfully, so I made some excuse and left him.

I filled in the rest of the afternoon by listening to talks which I could not understand and looking through microscopes at chromosomes and trying to persuade myself that I could do more than the professionals and see the genes, the original culprits who were responsible for the fact that all men were not turned out on one model, like so many Woolworth bakelite salt-cellars.

A burly American gave me a lesson in evolution, expounding Darwin to such an extent that I felt that the *Origin of Species* was a simple little book, in Basic English, for the use of school children. I wrote down a lot of notes and made him correct them, and, not content with that, I made him stand by my shoulder while I wrote out the rough draft of my next day's article, titling it, in the correct journalistic overstatement, "Why We Are Human." It was a pretty poor article and I could not understand it all myself, so I have no idea what the readers of the *Daily Courier* made of it. I suppose they must have been ashamed to show their ignorance, for I certainly received no complaints from the paper.

I got back to the hotel before the others had arrived and I found Uncle John in his bedroom, stretched out on the vast sofa that ran along one wall. He had a piece of paper over his face and as he breathed it flapped up and down. Even he could not deny that he was asleep. I had to shake him by the shoulder before he opened his eyes and sat up, spilling sheets of paper all over the floor.

"So you wanted to be alone?" I enquired in a ferocious Garbo voice. Uncle John did not seem to be the least perturbed as he pushed the hair back from his forehead and scowled at me amiably.

"Havin' finished my work," he roared, trying to look dignified, "I naturally assumed that I would be justified in takin' a little rest, and I may say that I did not expect to be thus rudely awakened by a hooligan. I have solved the problem to which I referred earlier to-day. The jewels were stolen by the Italian secretary, who shot the waxbill with an airgun, from the bathroom window. I found three grains of snuff upon the wireless aerial and that informed me that I was right. No more will he walk the byways of the world, snafflin' pigeon's blood rubies and emeralds the size of walnuts. His mistake was to think that he could fool me. Once more the twin detectives, Eagle Eye and Dogsnose, have proved invincible. Let this be a warning to all crooks."

He thumped himself upon the chest and the contents of his pockets jangled and crackled. Then he looked more serious. "I think I deserve a little beer after that," he announced, and we went down to the bar. There we found the inspector, drinking mild and bitter, and Dr. Flanagan, with a glass of Jameson's Irish whiskey.

My Uncle John refused to talk about the murder during dinner and exchanged stories about his adventures as a student with Dr. Flanagan, while the inspector and I examined each other, if not neutrally, at least non-belligerently. It was only when we arrived at the stage of coffee and brandy that my uncle came round to the subject which was occupying all our minds.

"Humph," he snorted, blowing out a cloud of cigar smoke, "I suppose we'd better get to our murder. I am convinced that I know who killed Porter, and then, because he knew too much, Dr. Swartz. I think I could prove my case, but though it might satisfy me, I doubt very much whether it would satisfy you or a jury. So I have made arrangements for an experiment. In a few moments we will go up to my room, and the three of you will hide behind various things in the room while I sit at the table.

"No matter if Old Nick himself should appear in the room, I don't want any of you to disclose his presence until I give you the word, not even if you should think I am in danger. I am quite old enough to look after myself, and I want you to realise that I know what I'm doin'. You understand that you are not to make a sound, under any circumstances whatsoever? Yes? Then that's all right, but for God's sake don't forget your instructions in the heat of the moment.

"Now, I want you, Inspector Hargrave, and you, Joe, to leave the hotel by the front entrance and to walk along the street until you get to the corner of Norval Terrace. Turn down there and then come back to the hotel and come in by the servants' entrance. I don't expect anyone will stop you but if someone should, you can show them your card and impress upon them the need for secrecy. Come up to my floor—you know where it is? Good—in the service-lift—not, under any circumstances, by the stairs. Then you can join me in my room and I'll hide you. Got all that? Good. Then you can go."

The inspector and doctor, giving what I thought was a very poor display of nonchalance, left the room. My uncle turned to me, "You heard my instructions? That's fine. Now, we'll give them five minutes' start and then I want you to do exactly the same. If anyone happens to be watching the hotel, that person will, I hope, think that I have been left alone and will act on that assumption."

He filled up my glass and I drank it slowly, keeping my eye on my wrist-watch. Uncle John rose to his feet and pressed the butt of his cigar into the ash-tray and I walked down the room beside him. He accompanied me to the door of the hotel and boomed, "I'll see you about ten-thirty then, Andrew. See if you can do that for me."

As I walked down the street I felt that someone had taken a plane and shaved the inside of my stomach. Anyone who was watching me would have got the impression that I was slightly drunk, for my legs seemed to respond very slowly to my wishes and I bounced slightly off the shoulders of passers-by, who looked at me with faint distaste. I saw no one I knew, which, I thought, was just as well for my reputation.

However, by the time I had reached the back door of the hotel I had managed to get my wilful body more or less under control. No one stopped me and I had little difficulty in locating the service lift.

The others were already in the room with my uncle. I reached for my packet of cigarettes, but he put out his hand. "Sorry, Andrew, I'm the only one who can smoke here." He waved his cigar. "It might give the game away if even one cigarette-end was to be left about this room. I have no doubt that our murderer has observed that I only smoke cigars and my pipe."

He fanned out his papers on the table in the centre of the room and pulled a light armchair up to it, laying his landing net against it so that the handle lay beside the arm. He looked at his turnip-watch and, like a general marshalling his troops, gestured us into different parts of the room. "I want you, Andrew, to get into that wardrobe. I bored a small hole at your eye level this afternoon and fixed a bar across inside, so that there's no fear of the doors swinging open suddenly if you lean on it, but all the same I'd rather you didn't lean as it might creak. You, Inspector, get down behind the sofa. I'm afraid you'll find it a tight fit but I daren't pull it any further away from the wall, as it might be noticeable, and Joe, you are the lightest of us, so you'd better get on top of the wardrobe."

We gave the little doctor a leg up and made certain that he was not visible to anyone entering the room. Then the inspector and I took up our positions.

My uncle had very thoughtfully thrown all his clothes on to the floor of the cupboard, so that I had something soft to stand on and was not troubled by having them clinging about my neck and shoulders. I found I could see out quite clearly through my peep-hole. Uncle John was seated at the table, writing with a perfectly steady hand. Every now and again he leaned back and drew appreciatively at his cigar and blew a careful smoke-ring. He looked as though he had not a care in the world and felt quite at home in the part of the innocent goat playing bait for the very fierce tiger.

I do not, of course, know how the others felt, but there was an extremely heavy weight inside me which insisted upon bouncing up and down in my stomach, and I could do absolutely nothing to steady it. My mouth was dry and there was a curious sound of singing in my ears, like a legion of distant kettles, or, as one of my eighteenth-century letter-writers put it, "like meat fryed in pan."

Quite suddenly the weight settled in the pit of my stomach and the noise in my ears stopped. Short brisk steps were advancing along the passage, their crispness sounding on the linoleum-covered floor. The steps came to a stop for a moment and whoever was outside the door paused. Then the door handle turned sharply. I do not know why I did, but I shut my eyes.

CHAPTER 2

POP GOES THE WEASEL

WHEN I looked out of my peep-hole again I almost shouted with relief. Where I had expected to see a murderer I saw a girl. My uncle's visitor was Mary Lewis. I was just on the point of lifting the bar that held my door shut when I remembered my uncle's instructions that we were not to come out of our hiding places for any reason whatsoever, and I decided I had better stay where I was. I chuckled silently to myself as I thought how I would mystify Mary later by giving her details of her interview with my uncle.

She looked quickly round the room and then, apparently satisfied, remarked cheerfully, "I think you wanted to see me, Professor Stubbs."

My uncle waved his cigar in a leisurely manner and grunted. "Umhum." He waved towards a chair on the other side of the table. "Won't you sit down?"

"No, I think I'd rather stand. What do you want to see me about? I've only got a few minutes before I meet Peter."

He sighed heavily. "I know who murdered Porter and Dr. Swartz," he rumbled suddenly, and his voice sounded curiously empty. He slid a sheet of paper across towards her and she picked it up. She looked at it for a moment and then took a handkerchief out of her bag and dabbed at her nose with it. "This is really too ridiculous, Professor Stubbs," she said, and her laugh seemed completely undisturbed. "Why should *I* murder first Dr. Porter and then Dr. Swartz. Neither of them meant that much to me." She flicked her fingers.

Good God, I thought, poor old Uncle John's making a fool of himself all right. It's just as well that Mary does not know that he has hidden witnesses all round the room, because if she did she could probably get whacking great damages out of him for slander.

He did not seem to be the least disturbed by her laughter. "Humm," he said slowly, "I don't want to go into it all here but I rather fancy that you'd been havin' a little affair with Dr. Ian Porter to console you for the absence of Peter Hatton, and though you had finished with Porter he had not finished with you and refused to let go. I don't think you cared a damn about him and his threats, but I think that you realised that he could do one thing. He could make you a figure of fun and he could presume upon his past and your past, to remain unduly familiar."

Mary stood opposite my uncle, playing with her handkerchief. His words did not seem to worry her unduly, but I thought I detected a sultry look at the corners of her mouth and on her temples, which showed that she would soon lose her temper and tell Uncle John where he got off.

"You laid your plans pretty carefully," he went on, "and I dare say you thought that they had been properly wrecked when Peter walked in and slammed Porter on the chin. However, you are fairly quick-witted and you managed to anger the already furious Peter still further, so that he walked out, leaving you alone with the unconscious figure of Porter. Then it seemed to you that this was even better than your original plan and would require less time to carry out. So you jabbed your hypodermic syringe, which you had previously bought when the idea of murdering Porter first occurred to you, into his ear, set the stage quickly and rushed out to the lavatory. I don't think that you returned again, but made up the story of your return so that we would think your openness a very strong point in your favour.

"The plan was very clever, very good as a bit of slapdash scenery painting, but you made one very bad mistake. Among the red herrin's you arranged was a taste-test half-filled in. I had a very interesting conversation with young Stuart this afternoon, during which he informed me that you had done the taste-test earlier in the morning and had then left it with him to check up while you went to show someone their blood-group. If you had waited to hear his comments on your sheet you would not have made your mistake.

"You filled in the sheet with your own tastes, thinkin' by this to make it look plausible. You did not realise that you had a peculiarity which gave you away, and you copied this peculiarity on to the sheet you left by Porter's body."

Mary still fiddled with her handkerchief and she still did not seem to be in the least perturbed by my uncle's accusations. I felt that she must know that she had some pretty good answer to them.

"Swartz," Uncle John went on heavily, "noticed that there was somethin' funny about the papers when he explained them to the inspector and he cabled to America for Porter's reactions to the taste-test. When the answer to the cable arrived he realised that he was right and rang you up, sayin' that he wanted you to explain somethin' about the death of Porter. He must have let his suspicions show in his voice for you immediately suggested that you should talk it over with him and suggested Dr. Fielding's room, as you knew it was well away from the places where people would be in the evenin'.

"Naturally, you knew all about the room, for Peter was workin' there and what could be more natural than that you should drop in to see him occasionally? Dr. Swartz might be suspicious of you, but he would be on his guard against guile, not against force, and so you decided that as you were a fairly strong girl you would take him by surprise.

"Again your plan was slap-dash, like a badly dusted room, where the cobwebs remain in the corners and under the carpet. You had not sufficient time to make up your plan, but you did the best you could on the spur of the moment, tellin' Peter that you had to meet an old girl-friend and that he'd find the Gene Group more to his taste than the cluckin' of a couple of hens. Peter obediently went to the Gene Group and left at the same time as Swartz. He was to be your alibi on the front door, to see you arrivin' in a hurry, desperately sorry for being so late, but of course he would understand what it was like when two girls who had not seen each other for ages got together, and so on. He swallowed this, as you knew he would, rod, line and sinker, or whatever the sayin' is.

"You then, with the same lack of economy you'd shown in the murder of Porter, proceeded to eliminate Dr. Swartz, without a regret. All that mattered to you was your safety and you were going to obtain that, no matter how many people you had to kill in the process."

Mary laughed at him and said softly, her tone that of one who is mildly amused, "My dear Professor Stubbs, do you really imagine that this fairy tale has any basis in fact or that anyone would believe it? Can you imagine a jury taking it all in? I think you're a perfectly sweet old thing, but you'll never make a detective. You spin a tale like this and you haven't an atom of proof with which to back it up."

My uncle finished filling his pipe and stuck it into the corner of his mouth. He lit one of his fusees and the sulphurous glare made his face look like that of a corpse. "Umhum, I don't suppose I do appear to have very much proof at the moment," he said, letting each word down heavily like pebbles down the mouth of the well, "but on the other hand, there are certain things you will have to explain, and one of these is the absence of your girl friend." He sucked heavily at his pipe. "Another... *suck*... is why... *suck*... one of your... *puff*... finger-prints... *suck*... appears on the bowl of Swartz's pipe—the polished corn-cob took a good impression."

He paused and Mary's mouth dropped open. She looked at his face but it was as immovable as the face of one of those Graeco Buddhist stone statues. "What's that?" she demanded furiously.

Uncle John blew a cloud of sparks from his pipe and said, "You left one of your finger-prints on the bowl of Swartz's pipe."

"That's a lie," she almost screamed. "I couldn't have... I wore rubber gloves... Oh." She paused, realising what she had said and pulled herself together.

"Well, then," she said coolly, "supposing I did do the murders, what then? I might have left the finger-print on Dr. Swartz's pipe hours before. He sometimes laid it down on the table and I might have handed it to him. It's only your word against mine, and that wouldn't count for much in a court of law. A good lawyer would have no difficulty in showing you up as a romancing old man."

Inside the cupboard I felt rotten, the air was getting very stuffy, and in spite of the scene outside I was finding it difficult to keep my eyes open. I placed my hand on the bar so as to ready to lift it as soon as my uncle spoke, and, concentrating hard, I peeped out of the hole. Mary had moved round the table as she spoke and she was again fumbling with her handkerchief, putting it away in her bag, which lay on the table in front of her. I noticed that my uncle's hand was hanging over the arm of the chair. As I watched him he gripped the handle.

Mary, having stowed her handkerchief in the bag, was taking her hand out. At that moment my uncle swept up his net and clapped it down over the bag and her hand so hard that she yelped with pain as the aluminium rim struck her wrist. "You can come out now," he roared.

I heaved up the bar which was holding the wardrobe door shut and stumbled out into the room, drawing a deep breath as I did so. The inspector, however, was even quicker than I was, and had squirmed out from behind the sofa and grabbed Mary from behind by the elbows. She fought like a lynx and one of her nails ripped a strip of skin down the side of my face. However, my uncle had swept his net and catch across the table out of reach, so that she could not get at any weapons which she had concealed there. As the inspector and I struggled with her I saw Dr. Flanagan climbing down from the top of the wardrobe.

Before he reached us she succeeded in giving me a worse hacking on the shins than I had ever expected to find outside the Rugby played by teams in the borders of Scotland. The doctor threw himself at her legs and the three of us managed to bear her backwards to the couch. Quite suddenly, she stopped struggling and Inspector Hargrave snapped his handcuffs over her wrists, and administered the official warning.

She looked at them disdainfully. "It's all right," she said scornfully, "I know when I'm beaten, even if it takes three men to do it. You've got me and I suppose you'll do your best to hang me. Porter got what he was asking for, and as for Dr. Swartz, he should have kept his nose out of other people's business. And so should that old bastard."

She jangled the cuffs in the direction of my uncle, who paid no attention but lifted his fishing net and explored the contents of her bag. He took out her handkerchief, and, with it covering his finger and thumb, withdrew a hypodermic syringe, which he raised gingerly towards his nose.

"I always did say there was too much cyanide about this case," he remarked peevishly as he laid it down gingerly and relighted his pipe. When he had completed this ceremony, he emptied out the contents of the bag upon the table and looked through for odds and ends, examining a lipstick as if half afraid that it might explode in his face, opening it up and shaking it.

He placed one or two little things, a bottle of pills and a pair of nail scissors, to one side, ran his fingers round inside the bag to see that he had not missed anything, and then replaced such oddments as appeared to be harmless. He snapped the bag shut and handed it back to Mary with a bow. "I am afraid that I have had to remove any things that might be lethal."

Mary, limp and listless, looked at him and then at the inspector. "Inspector Hargrave," she said, "I would like you to allow me to do my face before you take me to the police station. Do you mind?"

The inspector looked a little startled at this request, and scratched his head as if trying to remember whether there was any clause in the regulations which dealt with the matter. He did not seem to remember one and growled, "All right, but be quick about it and, mind now, no funny stuff."

She smiled up at him, as sweetly as she had ever smiled at Peter, and, slightly hindered by the handcuffs, juggled a powder-puff, her mirror and lipstick out of the bag. As she powdered her nose carefully and drew a careful line along her lips, I watched her closely, noticing that her hand was as steady as it had been when taking the drop of blood from my ear. I shuddered slightly as I thought of that drop of blood.

She finished her lips and looked at them critically in the little mirror, and apparently deciding that they needed a little more making up, placed the stick of tawny orange against her lips. She opened her mouth and I thought she was going to say something. I glimpsed her strong white teeth as she closed them sharply on the lipstick. There was a crack of breaking glass and she choked slightly, smiled and slipped over sideways. I sniffed and recognised that curious bitter-sweet odour which, I hope, will never trouble my nose again as long as I live.

The inspector looked down incredulously. The deep voice of my Uncle John boomed suddenly. "Don't look so depressed, Inspector," he said. "All things considered, it's the best way. You could never have hoped to have proved a proper case against her, or, at least, not unless you could have found a great deal more than I know. We're all witnesses to the effect that you were in no way to blame. None of us could be expected to think of a glass-tube in her lipstick."

Dr. Flanagan looked up from his position bent over the body of Mary and scowled. "You old charlatan, John," he said bluntly, "I believe you knew." My uncle paid no attention but gave the inspector the hypodermic syringe. The inspector went over to the telephone beside the bed and lifted the receiver. His back was turned to us. Uncle John pushed his big face close to the doctor's ear and whispered hoarsely, "Can't you hold your tongue, Joe. It's the best way. Leave well enough alone."

A wintry smile creased the little doctor's cheeks and he nodded. "One of these days, John," he remarked with the air of one reciting a proverb, "you'll pick your firework up by the wrong end."

CHAPTER 3

EASY COME EASY GO

AFTER THE POLICE had finished with us, my uncle, having pacified the hotel manager, and, funking the job himself, having sent a police officer to find Peter and explain matters to him, ordered tankards of beer and we sat down to drink it. I do not think that beer ever tasted so good before! I had not realised that my mouth felt as though I had been drinking woolly tea out of one of the surrealist's fur tea-cups.

The inspector, smoking a cigar as delicately as if it was made of dynamite, looked over to my uncle, who had spread himself over the sofa. "Come on, now, Professor," he urged politely, "tell us about it. I'm willing to admit you put a fast one over on us." He paused and then went on. "By the way, it may interest you to know that Silver's alibi could, probably have been broken. At the end of his corridor in the hostel, which, as you probably know, is one of those huge old-fashioned houses remodelled, there is a stair which is only used by the servants for carrying coal and so forth. Silver was not seen to enter the hostel by anyone when Porter was murdered and then, at about the time that Swartz was murdered, he was, presumably, locked in his room, having warned the servants that he was going to work and would not answer any knocks on the door. I was going to concentrate closer on the times and see if he could be the murderer. You see, the trouble was that no one had a proper alibi."

Uncle John took a pull at his tankard and placed it carefully on the floor. His voice echoed in the silent room as he spoke.

"That," he said, "was the whole trouble. As a reader of detective stories I know all about the murder done in the room where only the victim could have been—all bolts fastened on the inside—and where every suspect has a seemingly perfect alibi. This case was the exact opposite of the closed box mystery. Here anyone could have done the murder and we had to make up our minds as to which people, out of the odd two thousand attendin' this Congress, could have done it.

"Once we swept away the red herrin's, the glassful of cyanide, the broken dropper, and so on, and discovered how the murder had been committed, we saw that it narrowed the suspects down to those who were intimate enough with Porter to be asked to take a drop of blood from his ear, and who also knew that he intended to work there durin' the lunch-hour. Now, those who knew that Porter intended to work in the demonstration room were Swartz, Andrew Blake, Mary Lewis, Peter Hatton, the two assistants, and, presumably, Silver. Of these there was only one person who could not have committed the murder as originally planned, and that person was Andrew Blake. If you want to know the reason for this, I can supply it in the form of a question—would any of you allow anyone but a doctor or surgeon to perform an operation on you?"

He looked round at this triumphantly and we shook our heads slowly. I felt rather as if I was eavesdropping, listening to myself being discussed in the third person.

"No, of course you wouldn't. Well, can you imagine Porter asking Andrew, whom he knew to be a journalist, to help him in a scientific experiment? Of the remainder, Swartz was a doubtful quantity. He had a reason for killin' Porter and, by his own account, he had the opportunity. The murderer had obviously made arrangement to get hold of Porter alone and Swartz hadn't done this—how was he to know that Powys wouldn't come lookin' for him?

"That left Peter Hatton, Silver and Mary Lewis. Peter admitted that he had knocked out Porter, and I considered that, if he did a murder, it would most likely be one of the blunt-instrument variety. But he could not be completely eliminated, as the method might be a display of cleverness, to put us off his track. However, I put him aside for the time bein' and concentrated on Silver and Mary Lewis.

"Either of them seemed to fulfil the necessary requirements. Silver was Porter's only real friend and would, no doubt, know all about his plans, and part of his loose alibi confirmed this. The janitor heard him chattin' with Porter as he left. The mere fact that in this absolute welter of alibiless people, one person should have an alibi made me suspicious of him—though it should also ha' made me suspicious o' meself.

"However, I did not think that I should fix upon one suspect more than another, so giving Silver one star on my list I moved on to look at Mary Lewis. Perhaps I am prejudicial as I have never liked her very much, but I looked over her case very carefully and, I *think*, without lettin' me prejudice rule me.

"Of all the suspects it seemed to me that she was the most likely. She worked with Porter, therefore she would know that he was workin' on a new non-coagulant and he would be quite likely to ask her to help him in an experiment. She would also know that he was bringing his materials with him and probably intended to give a demonstration when he had fixed them up.

"Then, again, I could not understand the undercurrent of familiarity

that ran between her and Porter. While I was puzzling over this I
suddenly remembered the case of Madeleine Smith—that's the *Notable Trial* clue I gave you, Inspector. I wondered whether, by any
chance, Porter could 'a taken the place of the unfortunate young
Frenchman.

"I must admit that I was going rather far in assumin' that this was
indeed the cause of the whole affair, but I assumed it, as I might say,
for the sake of argument, and the fragments began to fit into place like
those bits you never expect to fit into a jigsaw puzzle.

"There is no need for me to reconstruct the crime again. You all of
you heard what I said to her. Well, by this time I had a pretty sound
idea of the murderer, but I had no way of proving my case."

He drank the rest of his beer and rang the bell to order more.
When he had wiped the froth of the new tankard from his moustache
he went on.

"Then, of course, you arrested Andrew and I was too dam' clever. I
put you on to Swartz instead of Mary Lewis and Swartz died. This was
to a great extent my fault. If I had not wished to keep the murderer to
myself until I was certain I might have prevented it.

"When I found Swartz's body I realised that he must have found
some clue which had escaped my attention and the murderer must
have taken fright. I went back over everything and remembered the
red herrin's. Among these fish a sheet of paper stood out clearly. I
decided that I had better see it and see if the clue lay there. I
remembered that Andrew had given me two hints without realisin' it.
He had told me that Swartz had sent a cable to America and that there
had been two cases of an oddity in taste that mornin', the only two
which Swartz's assistant had encountered.

"Now, as we know, Porter had worked in America with Swartz,
when he was originally playin' about with his taste-testin', so that
Swartz would, presumably, have some idea of his tastin' peculiarities.
We knew, or assumed, that the paper had been filled up at random by
the murderer, but it occurred to me that Swartz would have immediately said that the paper was a random effort and so have destroyed
the effect of the stage settin'."

He looked over at the inspector. "When I went to your office this
morning, I copied out the tastes of Silver and Mary Lewis and one
odd one, just for the sake of safety. Then I sent Andrew to get a copy
of Swartz's cable, while I interviewed Swartz's assistant. He told me
that they juggled with the order of the glasses, so that memory could
play no part in someone's tastes if he went through the experiment
again, and he gave me the key to the lists I had collected.

"Andrew had managed to persuade," he emphasised the word gently, "the Western Union people to give him the cable and so, with that and my copies of the forms, I came back here and put in some hard work. The result of this was that I found that Mary's tastes coincided with those on the form by Porter's body, and it didn't seem likely that someone had filled the form up by accident. I don't like coincidences and so I assumed that Mary had filled the form herself."

The inspector was looking puzzled so my uncle heaved himself out of the couch and lumbered over to the table. He ruffled the papers and pulled out a sheet which he laid out flat. We leaned over the table and looked at it.

Uncle John picked up a pencil and scribbled on the back of an envelope as he spoke. "In this plan the tick is the correct answer, while X stands for Porter's taste, and √ is the taste on both Mary Lewis's paper and on the sheet found beside Porter's body. You will notice one striking peculiarity about this. She tastes all "sours" as sweet. Well, Andrew here did exactly the same, which surprised Swartz's assistant, who told me this afternoon that the chances against someone having that peculiarity and the other variations exactly the same was nearly astronomical. Andrew, for instance, in spite o' it, tasted nearly all the others right."

He laid down the pencil and lowered himself into the sofa. He scowled fiercely at the inspector. "Oh, I know that's not much use as evidence, but I didn't see that there was much chance of getting

	BITTER	BRACKISH	SOUR	SALT	SWEET	TASTELESS
A			X		√	
B	√	X				
C				X		√
D	X	√				
E			X		√	
F		X √				
G	X √					

more, so I arranged this little play for you, hopin' that I could manage to get some sort of admission or even an attack upon myself, that would bolster up what I had already found. I couldn't see a jury followin' that bit of paper. You remember what happened to Madeleine Smith. She got off on a non-proven which has been described as a verdict of 'Guilty but don't do it again.' Well, as there is no such verdict in England, Mary Lewis might have got 'Not guilty,' and I have little doubt but that, if she got tired of Peter, she'd 'a poisoned him too."

He pulled out his pipe and stuck it in his mouth. "Well, since you see where we are, and everything seems to be for the best in this worst of all possible worlds, and any other cliches you like, how about one more pint before we disperse for the night. Humph?"

A CATALOG OF SELECTED
DOVER BOOKS
IN ALL FIELDS OF INTEREST

A CATALOG OF SELECTED
DOVER BOOKS
IN ALL FIELDS OF INTEREST

DRAWINGS OF REMBRANDT, edited by Seymour Slive. Updated Lippmann, Hofstede de Groot edition, with definitive scholarly apparatus. All portraits, biblical sketches, landscapes, nudes. Oriental figures, classical studies, together with selection of work by followers. 550 illustrations. Total of 630pp. 9⅛ × 12¼.
21485-0, 21486-9 Pa., Two-vol. set $29.90

GHOST AND HORROR STORIES OF AMBROSE BIERCE, Ambrose Bierce. 24 tales vividly imagined, strangely prophetic, and decades ahead of their time in technical skill: "The Damned Thing," "An Inhabitant of Carcosa," "The Eyes of the Panther," "Moxon's Master," and 20 more. 199pp. 5⅜ × 8½. 20767-6 Pa. $4.95

ETHICAL WRITINGS OF MAIMONIDES, Maimonides. Most significant ethical works of great medieval sage, newly translated for utmost precision, readability. Laws Concerning Character Traits, Eight Chapters, more. 192pp. 5⅜ × 8½.
24522-5 Pa. $5.95

THE EXPLORATION OF THE COLORADO RIVER AND ITS CANYONS, J. W. Powell. Full text of Powell's 1,000-mile expedition down the fabled Colorado in 1869. Superb account of terrain, geology, vegetation, Indians, famine, mutiny, treacherous rapids, mighty canyons, during exploration of last unknown part of continental U.S. 400pp. 5⅜ × 8½. 20094-9 Pa. $7.95

HISTORY OF PHILOSOPHY, Julián Marías. Clearest one-volume history on the market. Every major philosopher and dozens of others, to Existentialism and later. 505pp. 5⅜ × 8½. 21739-6 Pa. $9.95

ALL ABOUT LIGHTNING, Martin A. Uman. Highly readable nontechnical survey of nature and causes of lightning, thunderstorms, ball lightning, St. Elmo's Fire, much more. Illustrated. 192pp. 5⅜ × 8½. 25237-X Pa. $5.95

SAILING ALONE AROUND THE WORLD, Captain Joshua Slocum. First man to sail around the world, alone, in small boat. One of great feats of seamanship told in delightful manner. 67 illustrations. 294pp. 5⅜ × 8½. 20326-3 Pa. $4.95

LETTERS AND NOTES ON THE MANNERS, CUSTOMS AND CONDITIONS OF THE NORTH AMERICAN INDIANS, George Catlin. Classic account of life among Plains Indians: ceremonies, hunt, warfare, etc. 312 plates. 572pp. of text. 6⅛ × 9¼. 22118-0, 22119-9, Pa., Two-vol. set $17.90

THE SECRET LIFE OF SALVADOR DALÍ, Salvador Dalí. Outrageous but fascinating autobiography through Dalí's thirties with scores of drawings and sketches and 80 photographs. A must for lovers of 20th-century art. 432pp. 6½ × 9¼. (Available in U.S. only)
27454-3 Pa. $9.95

THE BOOK OF BEASTS: Being a Translation from a Latin Bestiary of the Twelfth Century, T. H. White. Wonderful catalog of real and fanciful beasts: manticore, griffin, phoenix, amphivius, jaculus, many more. White's witty erudite commentary on scientific, historical aspects enhances fascinating glimpse of medieval mind. Illustrated. 296pp. 5⅜ × 8¼. (Available in U.S. only)   24609-4 Pa. $7.95

FRANK LLOYD WRIGHT: Architecture and Nature with 160 Illustrations, Donald Hoffmann. Profusely illustrated study of influence of nature—especially prairie—on Wright's designs for Fallingwater, Robie House, Guggenheim Museum, other masterpieces. 96pp. 9¼ × 10¾.   25098-9 Pa. $8.95

FRANK LLOYD WRIGHT'S FALLINGWATER, Donald Hoffmann. Wright's famous waterfall house: planning and construction of organic idea. History of site, owners, Wright's personal involvement. Photographs of various stages of building. Preface by Edgar Kaufmann, Jr. 100 illustrations. 112pp. 9¼ × 10.
23671-4 Pa. $8.95

YEARS WITH FRANK LLOYD WRIGHT: Apprentice to Genius, Edgar Tafel. Insightful memoir by a former apprentice presents a revealing portrait of Wright the man, the inspired teacher, the greatest American architect. 372 black-and-white illustrations. Preface. Index. vi + 228pp. 8¼ × 11.   24801-1 Pa. $10.95

THE STORY OF KING ARTHUR AND HIS KNIGHTS, Howard Pyle. Enchanting version of King Arthur fable has delighted generations with imaginative narratives of exciting adventures and unforgettable illustrations by the author. 41 illustrations. xviii + 313pp. 6⅛ × 9¼.   21445-1 Pa. $6.95

THE GODS OF THE EGYPTIANS, E. A. Wallis Budge. Thorough coverage of numerous gods of ancient Egypt by foremost Egyptologist. Information on evolution of cults, rites and gods; the cult of Osiris; the Book of the Dead and its rites; the sacred animals and birds; Heaven and Hell; and more. 956pp. 6⅛ × 9¼.
22055-9, 22056-7 Pa., Two-vol. set $21.90

A THEOLOGICO-POLITICAL TREATISE, Benedict Spinoza. Also contains unfinished *Political Treatise.* Great classic on religious liberty, theory of government on common consent. R. Elwes translation. Total of 421pp. 5⅜ × 8½.
20249-6 Pa. $7.95

INCIDENTS OF TRAVEL IN CENTRAL AMERICA, CHIAPAS, AND YUCATAN, John L. Stephens. Almost single-handed discovery of Maya culture; exploration of ruined cities, monuments, temples; customs of Indians. 115 drawings. 892pp. 5⅜ × 8½.   22404-X, 22405-8 Pa., Two-vol. set $17.90

LOS CAPRICHOS, Francisco Goya. 80 plates of wild, grotesque monsters and caricatures. Prado manuscript included. 183pp. 6⅜ × 9⅜.   22384-1 Pa. $6.95

AUTOBIOGRAPHY: The Story of My Experiments with Truth, Mohandas K. Gandhi. Not hagiography, but Gandhi in his own words. Boyhood, legal studies, purification, the growth of the Satyagraha (nonviolent protest) movement. Critical, inspiring work of the man who freed India. 480pp. 5⅜ × 8½. (Available in U.S. only)
24593-4 Pa. $6.95

CATALOG OF DOVER BOOKS

ILLUSTRATED DICTIONARY OF HISTORIC ARCHITECTURE, edited by Cyril M. Harris. Extraordinary compendium of clear, concise definitions for over 5,000 important architectural terms complemented by over 2,000 line drawings. Covers full spectrum of architecture from ancient ruins to 20th-century Modernism. Preface. 592pp. 7½ × 9⅝. 24444-X Pa. $15.95

THE NIGHT BEFORE CHRISTMAS, Clement Moore. Full text, and woodcuts from original 1848 book. Also critical, historical material. 19 illustrations. 40pp. 4⅝ × 6. 22797-9 Pa. $2.50

THE LESSON OF JAPANESE ARCHITECTURE: 165 Photographs, Jiro Harada. Memorable gallery of 165 photographs taken in the 1930's of exquisite Japanese homes of the well-to-do and historic buildings. 13 line diagrams. 192pp. 8⅜ × 11¼. 24778-3 Pa. $10.95

THE AUTOBIOGRAPHY OF CHARLES DARWIN AND SELECTED LETTERS, edited by Francis Darwin. The fascinating life of eccentric genius composed of an intimate memoir by Darwin (intended for his children); commentary by his son, Francis; hundreds of fragments from notebooks, journals, papers; and letters to and from Lyell, Hooker, Huxley, Wallace and Henslow. xi + 365pp. 5⅜ × 8. 20479-0 Pa. $6.95

WONDERS OF THE SKY: Observing Rainbows, Comets, Eclipses, the Stars and Other Phenomena, Fred Schaaf. Charming, easy-to-read poetic guide to all manner of celestial events visible to the naked eye. Mock suns, glories, Belt of Venus, more. Illustrated. 299pp. 5¼ × 8¼. 24402-4 Pa. $7.95

BURNHAM'S CELESTIAL HANDBOOK, Robert Burnham, Jr. Thorough guide to the stars beyond our solar system. Exhaustive treatment. Alphabetical by constellation: Andromeda to Cetus in Vol. 1; Chamaeleon to Orion in Vol. 2; and Pavo to Vulpecula in Vol. 3. Hundreds of illustrations. Index in Vol. 3. 2,000pp. 6⅛ × 9¼. 23567-X, 23568-8, 23673-0 Pa., Three-vol. set $41.85

STAR NAMES: Their Lore and Meaning, Richard Hinckley Allen. Fascinating history of names various cultures have given to constellations and literary and folkloristic uses that have been made of stars. Indexes to subjects. Arabic and Greek names. Biblical references. Bibliography. 563pp. 5⅜ × 8½. 21079-0 Pa. $8.95

THIRTY YEARS THAT SHOOK PHYSICS: The Story of Quantum Theory, George Gamow. Lucid, accessible introduction to influential theory of energy and matter. Careful explanations of Dirac's anti-particles, Bohr's model of the atom, much more. 12 plates. Numerous drawings. 240pp. 5⅜ × 8½. 24895-X Pa. $5.95

CHINESE DOMESTIC FURNITURE IN PHOTOGRAPHS AND MEASURED DRAWINGS, Gustav Ecke. A rare volume, now affordably priced for antique collectors, furniture buffs and art historians. Detailed review of styles ranging from early Shang to late Ming. Unabridged republication. 161 black-and-white drawings, photos. Total of 224pp. 8⅜ × 11¼. (Available in U.S. only) 25171-3 Pa. $13.95

VINCENT VAN GOGH: A Biography, Julius Meier-Graefe. Dynamic, penetrating study of artist's life, relationship with brother, Theo, painting techniques, travels, more. Readable, engrossing. 160pp. 5⅜ × 8½. (Available in U.S. only) 25253-1 Pa. $4.95

HOW TO WRITE, Gertrude Stein. Gertrude Stein claimed anyone could understand her unconventional writing—here are clues to help. Fascinating improvisations, language experiments, explanations illuminate Stein's craft and the art of writing. Total of 414pp. 4⅝ × 6⅜. 23144-5 Pa. $6.95

ADVENTURES AT SEA IN THE GREAT AGE OF SAIL: Five Firsthand Narratives, edited by Elliot Snow. Rare true accounts of exploration, whaling, shipwreck, fierce natives, trade, shipboard life, more. 33 illustrations. Introduction. 353pp. 5⅜ × 8½. 25177-2 Pa. $8.95

THE HERBAL OR GENERAL HISTORY OF PLANTS, John Gerard. Classic descriptions of about 2,850 plants—with over 2,700 illustrations—includes Latin and English names, physical descriptions, varieties, time and place of growth, more. 2,706 illustrations. xlv + 1,678pp. 8½ × 12¼. 23147-X Cloth. $75.00

DOROTHY AND THE WIZARD IN OZ, L. Frank Baum. Dorothy and the Wizard visit the center of the Earth, where people are vegetables, glass houses grow and Oz characters reappear. Classic sequel to *Wizard of Oz*. 256pp. 5⅜ × 8. 24714-7 Pa. $5.95

SONGS OF EXPERIENCE: Facsimile Reproduction with 26 Plates in Full Color, William Blake. This facsimile of Blake's original "Illuminated Book" reproduces 26 full-color plates from a rare 1826 edition. Includes "The Tyger," "London," "Holy Thursday," and other immortal poems. 26 color plates. Printed text of poems. 48pp. 5¼ × 7. 24636-1 Pa. $3.95

SONGS OF INNOCENCE, William Blake. The first and most popular of Blake's famous "Illuminated Books," in a facsimile edition reproducing all 31 brightly colored plates. Additional printed text of each poem. 64pp. 5¼ × 7. 22764-2 Pa. $3.95

PRECIOUS STONES, Max Bauer. Classic, thorough study of diamonds, rubies, emeralds, garnets, etc.: physical character, occurrence, properties, use, similar topics. 20 plates, 8 in color. 94 figures. 659pp. 6⅛ × 9¼. 21910-0, 21911-9 Pa., Two-vol. set $15.90

ENCYCLOPEDIA OF VICTORIAN NEEDLEWORK, S. F. A. Caulfeild and Blanche Saward. Full, precise descriptions of stitches, techniques for dozens of needlecrafts—most exhaustive reference of its kind. Over 800 figures. Total of 679pp. 8⅛ × 11. Two volumes. Vol. 1 22800-2 Pa. $11.95
Vol. 2 22801-0 Pa. $11.95

THE MARVELOUS LAND OF OZ, L. Frank Baum. Second Oz book, the Scarecrow and Tin Woodman are back with hero named Tip, Oz magic. 136 illustrations. 287pp. 5⅜ × 8½. 20692-0 Pa. $5.95

WILD FOWL DECOYS, Joel Barber. Basic book on the subject, by foremost authority and collector. Reveals history of decoy making and rigging, place in American culture, different kinds of decoys, how to make them, and how to use them. 140 plates. 156pp. 7⅞ × 10¾. 20011-6 Pa. $8.95

HISTORY OF LACE, Mrs. Bury Palliser. Definitive, profusely illustrated chronicle of lace from earliest times to late 19th century. Laces of Italy, Greece, England, France, Belgium, etc. Landmark of needlework scholarship. 266 illustrations. 672pp. 6⅛ × 9¼. 24742-2 Pa. $14.95

ILLUSTRATED GUIDE TO SHAKER FURNITURE, Robert Meader. All furniture and appurtenances, with much on unknown local styles. 235 photos. 146pp. 9 × 12.
22819-3 Pa. $8.95

WHALE SHIPS AND WHALING: A Pictorial Survey, George Francis Dow. Over 200 vintage engravings, drawings, photographs of barks, brigs, cutters, other vessels. Also harpoons, lances, whaling guns, many other artifacts. Comprehensive text by foremost authority. 207 black-and-white illustrations. 288pp. 6 × 9.
24808-9 Pa. $9.95

THE BERTRAMS, Anthony Trollope. Powerful portrayal of blind self-will and thwarted ambition includes one of Trollope's most heartrending love stories. 497pp. 5⅜ × 8½.
25119-5 Pa. $9.95

ADVENTURES WITH A HAND LENS, Richard Headstrom. Clearly written guide to observing and studying flowers and grasses, fish scales, moth and insect wings, egg cases, buds, feathers, seeds, leaf scars, moss, molds, ferns, common crystals, etc.—all with an ordinary, inexpensive magnifying glass. 209 exact line drawings aid in your discoveries. 220pp. 5⅜ × 8½.
23330-8 Pa. $4.95

RODIN ON ART AND ARTISTS, Auguste Rodin. Great sculptor's candid, wide-ranging comments on meaning of art; great artists; relation of sculpture to poetry, painting, music; philosophy of life, more. 76 superb black-and-white illustrations of Rodin's sculpture, drawings and prints. 119pp. 8⅜ × 11¼.
24487-3 Pa. $7.95

FIFTY CLASSIC FRENCH FILMS, 1912–1982: A Pictorial Record, Anthony Slide. Memorable stills from Grand Illusion, Beauty and the Beast, Hiroshima, Mon Amour, many more. Credits, plot synopses, reviews, etc. 160pp. 8¼ × 11.
25256-6 Pa. $11.95

THE PRINCIPLES OF PSYCHOLOGY, William James. Famous long course complete, unabridged. Stream of thought, time perception, memory, experimental methods; great work decades ahead of its time. 94 figures. 1,391pp. 5⅜ × 8½.
20381-6, 20382-4 Pa., Two-vol. set $23.90

BODIES IN A BOOKSHOP, R. T. Campbell. Challenging mystery of blackmail and murder with ingenious plot and superbly drawn characters. In the best tradition of British suspense fiction. 192pp. 5⅜ × 8½.
24720-1 Pa. $4.95

CALLAS: PORTRAIT OF A PRIMA DONNA, George Jellinek. Renowned commentator on the musical scene chronicles incredible career and life of the most controversial, fascinating, influential operatic personality of our time. 64 black-and-white photographs. 416pp. 5⅜ × 8¼.
25047-4 Pa. $8.95

GEOMETRY, RELATIVITY AND THE FOURTH DIMENSION, Rudolph Rucker. Exposition of fourth dimension, concepts of relativity as Flatland characters continue adventures. Popular, easily followed yet accurate, profound. 141 illustrations. 133pp. 5⅜ × 8½.
23400-2 Pa. $4.95

HOUSEHOLD STORIES BY THE BROTHERS GRIMM, with pictures by Walter Crane. 53 classic stories—Rumpelstiltskin, Rapunzel, Hansel and Gretel, the Fisherman and his Wife, Snow White, Tom Thumb, Sleeping Beauty, Cinderella, and so much more—lavishly illustrated with original 19th century drawings. 114 illustrations. x + 269pp. 5⅜ × 8½.
21080-4 Pa. $4.95

SUNDIALS, Albert Waugh. Far and away the best, most thorough coverage of ideas, mathematics concerned, types, construction, adjusting anywhere. Over 100 illustrations. 230pp. 5⅜ × 8½. 22947-5 Pa. $5.95

PICTURE HISTORY OF THE NORMANDIE: With 190 Illustrations, Frank O. Braynard. Full story of legendary French ocean liner: Art Deco interiors, design innovations, furnishings, celebrities, maiden voyage, tragic fire, much more. Extensive text. 144pp. 8⅞ × 11¾. 25257-4 Pa. $10.95

THE FIRST AMERICAN COOKBOOK: A Facsimile of "American Cookery," 1796, Amelia Simmons. Facsimile of the first American-written cookbook published in the United States contains authentic recipes for colonial favorites—pumpkin pudding, winter squash pudding, spruce beer, Indian slapjacks, and more. Introductory Essay and Glossary of colonial cooking terms. 80pp. 5⅜ × 8½. 24710-4 Pa. $3.50

101 PUZZLES IN THOUGHT AND LOGIC, C. R. Wylie, Jr. Solve murders and robberies, find out which fishermen are liars, how a blind man could possibly identify a color—purely by your own reasoning! 107pp. 5⅜ × 8½. 20367-0 Pa. $2.95

ANCIENT EGYPTIAN MYTHS AND LEGENDS, Lewis Spence. Examines animism, totemism, fetishism, creation myths, deities, alchemy, art and magic, other topics. Over 50 illustrations. 432pp. 5⅜ × 8½. 26525-0 Pa. $8.95

ANTHROPOLOGY AND MODERN LIFE, Franz Boas. Great anthropologist's classic treatise on race and culture. Introduction by Ruth Bunzel. Only inexpensive paperback edition. 255pp. 5⅜ × 8½. 25245-0 Pa. $7.95

THE TALE OF PETER RABBIT, Beatrix Potter. The inimitable Peter's terrifying adventure in Mr. McGregor's garden, with all 27 wonderful, full-color Potter illustrations. 55pp. 4¼ × 5½. (Available in U.S. only) 22827-4 Pa. $1.75

THREE PROPHETIC SCIENCE FICTION NOVELS, H. G. Wells. *When the Sleeper Wakes, A Story of the Days to Come* and *The Time Machine* (full version). 335pp. 5⅜ × 8½. (Available in U.S. only) 20605-X Pa. $8.95

APICIUS COOKERY AND DINING IN IMPERIAL ROME, edited and translated by Joseph Dommers Vehling. Oldest known cookbook in existence offers readers a clear picture of what foods Romans ate, how they prepared them, etc. 49 illustrations. 301pp. 6⅛ × 9¼. 23563-7 Pa. $7.95

SHAKESPEARE LEXICON AND QUOTATION DICTIONARY, Alexander Schmidt. Full definitions, locations, shades of meaning of every word in plays and poems. More than 50,000 exact quotations. 1,485pp. 6½ × 9¼. 22726-X, 22727-8 Pa., Two-vol. set $31.90

THE WORLD'S GREAT SPEECHES, edited by Lewis Copeland and Lawrence W. Lamm. Vast collection of 278 speeches from Greeks to 1970. Powerful and effective models; unique look at history. 842pp. 5⅜ × 8½. 20468-5 Pa. $12.95

THE BLUE FAIRY BOOK, Andrew Lang. The first, most famous collection, with many familiar tales: Little Red Riding Hood, Aladdin and the Wonderful Lamp, Puss in Boots, Sleeping Beauty, Hansel and Gretel, Rumpelstiltskin; 37 in all. 138 illustrations. 390pp. 5⅜ × 8½. 21437-0 Pa. $6.95

THE STORY OF THE CHAMPIONS OF THE ROUND TABLE, Howard Pyle. Sir Launcelot, Sir Tristram and Sir Percival in spirited adventures of love and triumph retold in Pyle's inimitable style. 50 drawings, 31 full-page. xviii + 329pp. 6½ × 9¼. 21883-X Pa. $7.95

THE MYTHS OF THE NORTH AMERICAN INDIANS, Lewis Spence. Myths and legends of the Algonquins, Iroquois, Pawnees and Sioux with comprehensive historical and ethnological commentary. 36 illustrations. 5⅜ × 8½.
25967-6 Pa. $8.95

GREAT DINOSAUR HUNTERS AND THEIR DISCOVERIES, Edwin H. Colbert. Fascinating, lavishly illustrated chronicle of dinosaur research, 1820s to 1960. Achievements of Cope, Marsh, Brown, Buckland, Mantell, Huxley, many others. 384pp. 5¼ × 8¼. 24701-5 Pa. $7.95

THE TASTEMAKERS, Russell Lynes. Informal, illustrated social history of American taste 1850s-1950s. First popularized categories Highbrow, Lowbrow, Middlebrow. 129 illustrations. New (1979) afterword. 384pp. 6 × 9.
23993-4 Pa. $8.95

DOUBLE CROSS PURPOSES, Ronald A. Knox. A treasure hunt in the Scottish Highlands, an old map, unidentified corpse, surprise discoveries keep reader guessing in this cleverly intricate tale of financial skullduggery. 2 black-and-white maps. 320pp. 5⅜ × 8½. (Available in U.S. only) 25032-6 Pa. $6.95

AUTHENTIC VICTORIAN DECORATION AND ORNAMENTATION IN FULL COLOR: 46 Plates from "Studies in Design," Christopher Dresser. Superb full-color lithographs reproduced from rare original portfolio of a major Victorian designer. 48pp. 9¼ × 12¼. 25083-0 Pa. $7.95

PRIMITIVE ART, Franz Boas. Remains the best text ever prepared on subject, thoroughly discussing Indian, African, Asian, Australian, and, especially, Northern American primitive art. Over 950 illustrations show ceramics, masks, totem poles, weapons, textiles, paintings, much more. 376pp. 5⅜ × 8. 20025-6 Pa. $7.95

SIDELIGHTS ON RELATIVITY, Albert Einstein. Unabridged republication of two lectures delivered by the great physicist in 1920-21. *Ether and Relativity* and *Geometry and Experience*. Elegant ideas in nonmathematical form, accessible to intelligent layman. vi + 56pp. 5⅜ × 8½. 24511-X Pa. $3.95

THE WIT AND HUMOR OF OSCAR WILDE, edited by Alvin Redman. More than 1,000 ripostes, paradoxes, wisecracks: Work is the curse of the drinking classes, I can resist everything except temptation, etc. 258pp. 5⅜ × 8½. 20602-5 Pa. $4.95

ADVENTURES WITH A MICROSCOPE, Richard Headstrom. 59 adventures with clothing fibers, protozoa, ferns and lichens, roots and leaves, much more. 142 illustrations. 232pp. 5⅜ × 8½. 23471-1 Pa. $4.95

PLANTS OF THE BIBLE, Harold N. Moldenke and Alma L. Moldenke. Standard reference to all 230 plants mentioned in Scriptures. Latin name, biblical reference, uses, modern identity, much more. Unsurpassed encyclopedic resource for scholars, botanists, nature lovers, students of Bible. Bibliography. Indexes. 123 black-and-white illustrations. 384pp. 6 × 9. 25069-5 Pa. $8.95

FAMOUS AMERICAN WOMEN: A Biographical Dictionary from Colonial Times to the Present, Robert McHenry, ed. From Pocahontas to Rosa Parks, 1,035 distinguished American women documented in separate biographical entries. Accurate, up-to-date data, numerous categories, spans 400 years. Indices. 493pp. 6½ × 9¼. 24523-3 Pa. $10.95

THE FABULOUS INTERIORS OF THE GREAT OCEAN LINERS IN HISTORIC PHOTOGRAPHS, William H. Miller, Jr. Some 200 superb photographs capture exquisite interiors of world's great "floating palaces"—1890s to 1980s: *Titanic, Ile de France, Queen Elizabeth, United States, Europa,* more. Approx. 200 black-and-white photographs. Captions. Text. Introduction. 160pp. 8⅞ × 11¾. 24756-2 Pa. $9.95

THE GREAT LUXURY LINERS, 1927–1954: A Photographic Record, William H. Miller, Jr. Nostalgic tribute to heyday of ocean liners. 186 photos of *Ile de France, Normandie, Leviathan, Queen Elizabeth, United States,* many others. Interior and exterior views. Introduction. Captions. 160pp. 9 × 12. 24056-8 Pa. $12.95

A NATURAL HISTORY OF THE DUCKS, John Charles Phillips. Great landmark of ornithology offers complete detailed coverage of nearly 200 species and subspecies of ducks: gadwall, sheldrake, merganser, pintail, many more. 74 full-color plates, 102 black-and-white. Bibliography. Total of 1,920pp. 8⅝ × 11¼. 25141-1, 25142-X Cloth., Two-vol. set $100.00

THE SEAWEED HANDBOOK: An Illustrated Guide to Seaweeds from North Carolina to Canada, Thomas F. Lee. Concise reference covers 78 species. Scientific and common names, habitat, distribution, more. Finding keys for easy identification. 224pp. 5⅜ × 8½. 25215-9 Pa. $6.95

THE TEN BOOKS OF ARCHITECTURE: The 1755 Leoni Edition, Leon Battista Alberti. Rare classic helped introduce the glories of ancient architecture to the Renaissance. 68 black-and-white plates. 336pp. 8⅜ × 11¼. 25239-6 Pa. $14.95

MISS MACKENZIE, Anthony Trollope. Minor masterpieces by Victorian master unmasks many truths about life in 19th-century England. First inexpensive edition in years. 392pp. 5⅜ × 8½. 25201-9 Pa. $8.95

THE RIME OF THE ANCIENT MARINER, Gustave Doré, Samuel Taylor Coleridge. Dramatic engravings considered by many to be his greatest work. The terrifying space of the open sea, the storms and whirlpools of an unknown ocean, the ice of Antarctica, more—all rendered in a powerful, chilling manner. Full text. 38 plates. 77pp. 9¼ × 12. 22305-1 Pa. $4.95

THE EXPEDITIONS OF ZEBULON MONTGOMERY PIKE, Zebulon Montgomery Pike. Fascinating firsthand accounts (1805–6) of exploration of Mississippi River, Indian wars, capture by Spanish dragoons, much more. 1,088pp. 5⅜ × 8½. 25254-X, 25255-8 Pa., Two-vol. set $25.90

CATALOG OF DOVER BOOKS

A CONCISE HISTORY OF PHOTOGRAPHY: Third Revised Edition, Helmut Gernsheim. Best one-volume history—camera obscura, photochemistry, daguerreotypes, evolution of cameras, film, more. Also artistic aspects—landscape, portraits, fine art, etc. 281 black-and-white photographs. 26 in color. 176pp. 8⅜ × 11¼.
25128-4 Pa. $14.95

THE DORÉ BIBLE ILLUSTRATIONS, Gustave Doré. 241 detailed plates from the Bible: the Creation scenes, Adam and Eve, Flood, Babylon, battle sequences, life of Jesus, etc. Each plate is accompanied by the verses from the King James version of the Bible. 241pp. 9 × 12.
23004-X Pa. $9.95

WANDERINGS IN WEST AFRICA, Richard F. Burton. Great Victorian scholar/adventurer's invaluable descriptions of African tribal rituals, fetishism, culture, art, much more. Fascinating 19th-century account. 624pp. 5⅜ × 8½. 26890-X Pa. $12.95

HISTORIC HOMES OF THE AMERICAN PRESIDENTS, Second Revised Edition, Irvin Haas. Guide to homes occupied by every president from Washington to Bush. Visiting hours, travel routes, more. 175 photos. 160pp. 8¼ × 11.
26751-2 Pa. $9.95

THE HISTORY OF THE LEWIS AND CLARK EXPEDITION, Meriwether Lewis and William Clark, edited by Elliott Coues. Classic edition of Lewis and Clark's day-by-day journals that later became the basis for U.S. claims to Oregon and the West. Accurate and invaluable geographical, botanical, biological, meteorological and anthropological material. Total of 1,508pp. 5⅜ × 8½.
21268-8, 21269-6, 21270-X Pa., Three-vol. set $29.85

LANGUAGE, TRUTH AND LOGIC, Alfred J. Ayer. Famous, clear introduction to Vienna, Cambridge schools of Logical Positivism. Role of philosophy, elimination of metaphysics, nature of analysis, etc. 160pp. 5⅜ × 8½. (Available in U.S. and Canada only)
20010-8 Pa. $3.95

MATHEMATICS FOR THE NONMATHEMATICIAN, Morris Kline. Detailed, college-level treatment of mathematics in cultural and historical context, with numerous exercises. For liberal arts students. Preface. Recommended Reading Lists. Tables. Index. Numerous black-and-white figures. xvi + 641pp. 5⅜ × 8½.
24823-2 Pa. $11.95

HANDBOOK OF PICTORIAL SYMBOLS, Rudolph Modley. 3,250 signs and symbols, many systems in full; official or heavy commercial use. Arranged by subject. Most in Pictorial Archive series. 143pp. 8⅜ × 11. 23357-X Pa. $7.95

INCIDENTS OF TRAVEL IN YUCATAN, John L. Stephens. Classic (1843) exploration of jungles of Yucatan, looking for evidences of Maya civilization. Travel adventures, Mexican and Indian culture, etc. Total of 669pp. 5⅜ × 8½.
20926-1, 20927-X Pa., Two-vol. set $13.90

CATALOG OF DOVER BOOKS

DEGAS: An Intimate Portrait, Ambroise Vollard. Charming, anecdotal memoir by famous art dealer of one of the greatest 19th-century French painters. 14 black-and-white illustrations. Introduction by Harold L. Van Doren. 96pp. 5⅜ × 8½.
25131-4 Pa. $4.95

PERSONAL NARRATIVE OF A PILGRIMAGE TO AL-MADINAH AND MECCAH, Richard F. Burton. Great travel classic by remarkably colorful personality. Burton, disguised as a Moroccan, visited sacred shrines of Islam, narrowly escaping death. 47 illustrations. 959pp. 5⅜ × 8½.
21217-3, 21218-1 Pa., Two-vol. set $19.90

PHRASE AND WORD ORIGINS, A. H. Holt. Entertaining, reliable, modern study of more than 1,200 colorful words, phrases, origins and histories. Much unexpected information. 254pp. 5⅜ × 8½.
20758-7 Pa. $5.95

THE RED THUMB MARK, R. Austin Freeman. In this first Dr. Thorndyke case, the great scientific detective draws fascinating conclusions from the nature of a single fingerprint. Exciting story, authentic science. 320pp. 5⅜ × 8½. (Available in U.S. only)
25210-8 Pa. $6.95

AN EGYPTIAN HIEROGLYPHIC DICTIONARY, E. A. Wallis Budge. Monumental work containing about 25,000 words or terms that occur in texts ranging from 3000 B.C. to 600 A.D. Each entry consists of a transliteration of the word, the word in hieroglyphs, and the meaning in English. 1,314pp. 6⅜ × 10.
23615-3, 23616-1 Pa., Two-vol. set $35.90

THE COMPLEAT STRATEGYST: Being a Primer on the Theory of Games of Strategy, J. D. Williams. Highly entertaining classic describes, with many illustrated examples, how to select best strategies in conflict situations. Prefaces. Appendices. xvi + 268pp. 5⅜ × 8½.
25101-2 Pa. $6.95

THE ROAD TO OZ, L. Frank Baum. Dorothy meets the Shaggy Man, little Button-Bright and the Rainbow's beautiful daughter in this delightful trip to the magical Land of Oz. 272pp. 5⅜ × 8.
25208-6 Pa. $5.95

POINT AND LINE TO PLANE, Wassily Kandinsky. Seminal exposition of role of point, line, other elements in nonobjective painting. Essential to understanding 20th-century art. 127 illustrations. 192pp. 6½ × 9¼.
23808-3 Pa. $5.95

LADY ANNA, Anthony Trollope. Moving chronicle of Countess Lovel's bitter struggle to win for herself and daughter Anna their rightful rank and fortune— perhaps at cost of sanity itself. 384pp. 5⅜ × 8½.
24669-8 Pa. $8.95

EGYPTIAN MAGIC, E. A. Wallis Budge. Sums up all that is known about magic in Ancient Egypt: the role of magic in controlling the gods, powerful amulets that warded off evil spirits, scarabs of immortality, use of wax images, formulas and spells, the secret name, much more. 253pp. 5⅜ × 8½.
22681-6 Pa. $4.95

THE DANCE OF SIVA, Ananda Coomaraswamy. Preeminent authority unfolds the vast metaphysic of India: the revelation of her art, conception of the universe, social organization, etc. 27 reproductions of art masterpieces. 192pp. 5⅜ × 8½.
24817-8 Pa. $6.95

CATALOG OF DOVER BOOKS

CHRISTMAS CUSTOMS AND TRADITIONS, Clement A. Miles. Origin, evolution, significance of religious, secular practices. Caroling, gifts, yule logs, much more. Full, scholarly yet fascinating; non-sectarian. 400pp. 5⅜ × 8½.

23354-5 Pa. $7.95

THE HUMAN FIGURE IN MOTION, Eadweard Muybridge. More than 4,500 stopped-action photos, in action series, showing undraped men, women, children jumping, lying down, throwing, sitting, wrestling, carrying, etc. 390pp. 7⅞ × 10⅝.

20204-6 Cloth. $24.95

THE MAN WHO WAS THURSDAY, Gilbert Keith Chesterton. Witty, fast-paced novel about a club of anarchists in turn-of-the-century London. Brilliant social, religious, philosophical speculations. 128pp. 5⅜ × 8½. 25121-7 Pa. $3.95

A CÉZANNE SKETCHBOOK: Figures, Portraits, Landscapes and Still Lifes, Paul Cézanne. Great artist experiments with tonal effects, light, mass, other qualities in over 100 drawings. A revealing view of developing master painter, precursor of Cubism. 102 black-and-white illustrations. 144pp. 8¾ × 6⅝. 24790-2 Pa. $6.95

AN ENCYCLOPEDIA OF BATTLES: Accounts of Over 1,560 Battles from 1479 B.C. to the Present, David Eggenberger. Presents essential details of every major battle in recorded history, from the first battle of Megiddo in 1479 B.C. to Grenada in 1984. List of Battle Maps. New Appendix covering the years 1967–1984. Index. 99 illustrations. 544pp. 6½ × 9¼. 24913-1 Pa. $14.95

AN ETYMOLOGICAL DICTIONARY OF MODERN ENGLISH, Ernest Weekley. Richest, fullest work, by foremost British lexicographer. Detailed word histories. Inexhaustible. Total of 856pp. 6½ × 9¼.

21873-2, 21874-0 Pa., Two-vol. set $19.90

WEBSTER'S AMERICAN MILITARY BIOGRAPHIES, edited by Robert McHenry. Over 1,000 figures who shaped 3 centuries of American military history. Detailed biographies of Nathan Hale, Douglas MacArthur, Mary Hallaren, others. Chronologies of engagements, more. Introduction. Addenda. 1,033 entries in alphabetical order. xi + 548pp. 6½ × 9¼. (Available in U.S. only)

24758-9 Pa. $13.95

LIFE IN ANCIENT EGYPT, Adolf Erman. Detailed older account, with much not in more recent books: domestic life, religion, magic, medicine, commerce, and whatever else needed for complete picture. Many illustrations. 597pp. 5⅜ × 8½.

22632-8 Pa. $9.95

HISTORIC COSTUME IN PICTURES, Braun & Schneider. Over 1,450 costumed figures shown, covering a wide variety of peoples: kings, emperors, nobles, priests, servants, soldiers, scholars, townsfolk, peasants, merchants, courtiers, cavaliers, and more. 256pp. 8⅜ × 11¼. 23150-X Pa. $9.95

THE NOTEBOOKS OF LEONARDO DA VINCI, edited by J. P. Richter. Extracts from manuscripts reveal great genius; on painting, sculpture, anatomy, sciences, geography, etc. Both Italian and English. 186 ms. pages reproduced, plus 500 additional drawings, including studies for *Last Supper*, *Sforza* monument, etc. 860pp. 7⅞ × 10¾. (Available in U.S. only) 22572-0, 22573-9 Pa., Two-vol. set $35.90

CATALOG OF DOVER BOOKS

THE ART NOUVEAU STYLE BOOK OF ALPHONSE MUCHA: All 72 Plates from "Documents Decoratifs" in Original Color, Alphonse Mucha. Rare copyright-free design portfolio by high priest of Art Nouveau. Jewelry, wallpaper, stained glass, furniture, figure studies, plant and animal motifs, etc. Only complete one-volume edition. 80pp. 9⅜ × 12¼. 24044-4 Pa. $9.95

ANIMALS: 1,419 COPYRIGHT-FREE ILLUSTRATIONS OF MAMMALS, BIRDS, FISH, INSECTS, ETC., edited by Jim Harter. Clear wood engravings present, in extremely lifelike poses, over 1,000 species of animals. One of the most extensive pictorial sourcebooks of its kind. Captions. Index. 284pp. 9 × 12. 23766-4 Pa. $9.95

OBELISTS FLY HIGH, C. Daly King. Masterpiece of American detective fiction, long out of print, involves murder on a 1935 transcontinental flight—"a very thrilling story"—NY Times. Unabridged and unaltered republication of the edition published by William Collins Sons & Co. Ltd., London, 1935. 288pp. 5⅜ × 8½. (Available in U.S. only) 25036-9 Pa. $5.95

VICTORIAN AND EDWARDIAN FASHION: A Photographic Survey, Alison Gernsheim. First fashion history completely illustrated by contemporary photographs. Full text plus 235 photos, 1840–1914, in which many celebrities appear. 240pp. 6½ × 9¼. 24205-6 Pa. $8.95

THE ART OF THE FRENCH ILLUSTRATED BOOK, 1700–1914, Gordon N. Ray. Over 630 superb book illustrations by Fragonard, Delacroix, Daumier, Doré, Grandville, Manet, Mucha, Steinlen, Toulouse-Lautrec and many others. Preface. Introduction. 633 halftones. Indices of artists, authors & titles, binders and provenances. Appendices. Bibliography. 608pp. 8⅜ × 11¼. 25086-5 Pa. $24.95

THE WONDERFUL WIZARD OF OZ, L. Frank Baum. Facsimile in full color of America's finest children's classic. 143 illustrations by W. W. Denslow. 267pp. 5⅜ × 8½. 20691-2 Pa. $7.95

FOLLOWING THE EQUATOR: A Journey Around the World, Mark Twain. Great writer's 1897 account of circumnavigating the globe by steamship. Ironic humor, keen observations, vivid and fascinating descriptions of exotic places. 197 illustrations. 720pp. 5⅜ × 8½. 26113-1 Pa. $15.95

THE FRIENDLY STARS, Martha Evans Martin & Donald Howard Menzel. Classic text marshalls the stars together in an engaging, non-technical survey, presenting them as sources of beauty in night sky. 23 illustrations. Foreword. 2 star charts. Index. 147pp. 5⅜ × 8½. 21099-5 Pa. $3.95

FADS AND FALLACIES IN THE NAME OF SCIENCE, Martin Gardner. Fair, witty appraisal of cranks, quacks, and quackeries of science and pseudoscience: hollow earth, Velikovsky, orgone energy, Dianetics, flying saucers, Bridey Murphy, food and medical fads, etc. Revised, expanded In the Name of Science. "A very able and even-tempered presentation."—The New Yorker. 363pp. 5⅜ × 8. 20394-8 Pa. $6.95

ANCIENT EGYPT: ITS CULTURE AND HISTORY, J. E Manchip White. From pre-dynastics through Ptolemies: society, history, political structure, religion, daily life, literature, cultural heritage. 48 plates. 217pp. 5⅜ × 8½. 22548-8 Pa. $5.95

CATALOG OF DOVER BOOKS

SIR HARRY HOTSPUR OF HUMBLETHWAITE, Anthony Trollope. Incisive, unconventional psychological study of a conflict between a wealthy baronet, his idealistic daughter, and their scapegrace cousin. The 1870 novel in its first inexpensive edition in years. 250pp. 5⅜ × 8½. 24953-0 Pa. $6.95

LASERS AND HOLOGRAPHY, Winston E. Kock. Sound introduction to burgeoning field, expanded (1981) for second edition. Wave patterns, coherence, lasers, diffraction, zone plates, properties of holograms, recent advances. 84 illustrations. 160pp. 5⅜ × 8¼. (Except in United Kingdom) 24041-X Pa. $3.95

INTRODUCTION TO ARTIFICIAL INTELLIGENCE: Second, Enlarged Edition, Philip C. Jackson, Jr. Comprehensive survey of artificial intelligence—the study of how machines (computers) can be made to act intelligently. Includes introductory and advanced material. Extensive notes updating the main text. 132 black-and-white illustrations. 512pp. 5⅜ × 8½. 24864-X Pa. $10.95

HISTORY OF INDIAN AND INDONESIAN ART, Ananda K. Coomaraswamy. Over 400 illustrations illuminate classic study of Indian art from earliest Harappa finds to early 20th century. Provides philosophical, religious and social insights. 304pp. 6⅜ × 9⅜. 25005-9 Pa. $11.95

THE GOLEM, Gustav Meyrink. Most famous supernatural novel in modern European literature, set in Ghetto of Old Prague around 1890. Compelling story of mystical experiences, strange transformations, profound terror. 13 black-and-white illustrations. 224pp. 5⅜ × 8½. (Available in U.S. only) 25025-3 Pa. $6.95

PICTORIAL ENCYCLOPEDIA OF HISTORIC ARCHITECTURAL PLANS, DETAILS AND ELEMENTS: With 1,880 Line Drawings of Arches, Domes, Doorways, Facades, Gables, Windows, etc., John Theodore Haneman. Sourcebook of inspiration for architects, designers, others. Bibliography. Captions. 141pp. 9 × 12. 24605-1 Pa. $8.95

BENCHLEY LOST AND FOUND, Robert Benchley. Finest humor from early 30s, about pet peeves, child psychologists, post office and others. Mostly unavailable elsewhere. 73 illustrations by Peter Arno and others. 183pp. 5⅜ × 8½. 22410-4 Pa. $4.95

ERTÉ GRAPHICS, Erté. Collection of striking color graphics: *Seasons, Alphabet, Numerals, Aces* and *Precious Stones.* 50 plates, including 4 on covers. 48pp. 9⅜ × 12¼. 23580-7 Pa. $7.95

THE JOURNAL OF HENRY D. THOREAU, edited by Bradford Torrey, F. H. Allen. Complete reprinting of 14 volumes, 1837–61, over two million words; the sourcebooks for *Walden,* etc. Definitive. All original sketches, plus 75 photographs. 1,804pp. 8½ × 12¼. 20312-3, 20313-1 Cloth., Two-vol. set $130.00

CASTLES: Their Construction and History, Sidney Toy. Traces castle development from ancient roots. Nearly 200 photographs and drawings illustrate moats, keeps, baileys, many other features. Caernarvon, Dover Castles, Hadrian's Wall, Tower of London, dozens more. 256pp. 5⅜ × 8¼. 24898-4 Pa. $7.95

AMERICAN CLIPPER SHIPS: 1833–1858, Octavius T. Howe & Frederick C. Matthews. Fully-illustrated, encyclopedic review of 352 clipper ships from the period of America's greatest maritime supremacy. Introduction. 109 halftones. 5 black-and-white line illustrations. Index. Total of 928pp. 5⅜ × 8½.
25115-2, 25116-0 Pa., Two-vol. set $17.90

TOWARDS A NEW ARCHITECTURE, Le Corbusier. Pioneering manifesto by great architect, near legendary founder of "International School." Technical and aesthetic theories, views on industry, economics, relation of form to function, "mass-production spirit," much more. Profusely illustrated. Unabridged translation of 13th French edition. Introduction by Frederick Etchells. 320pp. 6⅛ × 9¼. (Available in U.S. only)
25023-7 Pa. $8.95

THE BOOK OF KELLS, edited by Blanche Cirker. Inexpensive collection of 32 full-color, full-page plates from the greatest illuminated manuscript of the Middle Ages, painstakingly reproduced from rare facsimile edition. Publisher's Note. Captions. 32pp. 9⅜ × 12¼. (Available in U.S. only)
24345-1 Pa. $5.95

BEST SCIENCE FICTION STORIES OF H. G. WELLS, H. G. Wells. Full novel *The Invisible Man*, plus 17 short stories: "The Crystal Egg," "Aepyornis Island," "The Strange Orchid," etc. 303pp. 5⅜ × 8½. (Available in U.S. only)
21531-8 Pa. $6.95

AMERICAN SAILING SHIPS: Their Plans and History, Charles G. Davis. Photos, construction details of schooners, frigates, clippers, other sailcraft of 18th to early 20th centuries—plus entertaining discourse on design, rigging, nautical lore, much more. 137 black-and-white illustrations. 240pp. 6⅛ × 9¼.
24658-2 Pa. $6.95

ENTERTAINING MATHEMATICAL PUZZLES, Martin Gardner. Selection of author's favorite conundrums involving arithmetic, money, speed, etc., with lively commentary. Complete solutions. 112pp. 5⅜ × 8½.
25211-6 Pa. $3.50

THE WILL TO BELIEVE, HUMAN IMMORTALITY, William James. Two books bound together. Effect of irrational on logical, and arguments for human immortality. 402pp. 5⅜ × 8½.
20291-7 Pa. $8.95

THE HAUNTED MONASTERY and THE CHINESE MAZE MURDERS, Robert Van Gulik. 2 full novels by Van Gulik continue adventures of Judge Dee and his companions. An evil Taoist monastery, seemingly supernatural events; overgrown topiary maze that hides strange crimes. Set in 7th-century China. 27 illustrations. 328pp. 5⅜ × 8½.
23502-5 Pa. $6.95

CELEBRATED CASES OF JUDGE DEE (DEE GOONG AN), translated by Robert Van Gulik. Authentic 18th-century Chinese detective novel; Dee and associates solve three interlocked cases. Led to Van Gulik's own stories with same characters. Extensive introduction. 9 illustrations. 237pp. 5⅜ × 8½.
23337-5 Pa. $5.95

Prices subject to change without notice.

Available at your book dealer or write for free catalog to Dept. GI, Dover Publications, Inc., 31 East 2nd St., Mineola, N.Y. 11501. Dover publishes more than 175 books each year on science, elementary and advanced mathematics, biology, music, art, literary history, social sciences and other areas.